The Conspiracies of

by SANDRA BIBER DIDNER

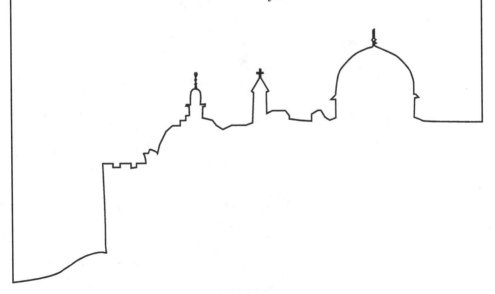

Scan this QR Code
to learn more about
this title

Cover and interior design by Emily Dueker
Necklace with the Star of David © Andrea Santini. Dreamstime.com.
Old City Jerusalem © Crazy80Frog. Dreamstime.com.
Jerusalem Skyline © Emily Dueker

Publisher: Inkwater Press | www.inkwaterpress.com

Paperback
ISBN-13 978-1-59299-784-8 | ISBN-10 1-59299-784-8

Kindle
ISBN-13 978-1-59299-785-5 | ISBN-10 1-59299-785-6

ePub
ISBN-13 978-1-59299-786-2 | ISBN-10 1-59299-786-4

Printed in the U.S.A.
All paper is acid free and meets all ANSI standards for archival quality paper.

5 7 9 10 8 6 4 2

Dedicated to David and Hannah,
Rebecca and Ishmael,
the donkey and her children.
This is their story.

Man is but an ass if he go about to expound this dream...
It shall be called "Bottom's Dream," because it hath no bottom.

A Midsummer Night's Dream by William Shakespeare

PROLOGUE

Palés

THE SEARCH

ISRAEL, MAY 1979

The discouraged donkey plods along the dusty road followed by her three weary foals. She has no idea where home is. Once, she used to know when she was worshipped as the mischievous Palés, the fertility goddess. Her people, the Sumerians, the Akkadians, the Syrians, the Canaanites, the Amorites, the Hittites, and the Jebusites, loved her and prayed to her when they wanted children. The Romans, however, exalted her and held a feast day, the Parilia, in her honor on April 21. They built her temple in the most important part of Rome named especially for her: The Palatine Hill. She knows they named Palestine after her as well, although the Philistines tried to take that honor away from her. Historians, who think they know everything, falsely claim that the land is named after the sea trading Philistines. But the donkey remembers when these traders who lived in the cities of Gaza and Ashkelon, and the Hebrews who lived beside them in the land of Canaan were taken captive by the Babylonians. Both peoples were exiled to the land people today call Iraq, but her worshippers called Urak long before the Romans conquered the Middle East.

When the Roman Empire fell, the Muslims, Christians, and Jews converted the pagan goddess into a beast of burden. Through the millennia she carried them on her back, toted their goods, and, together with the horse, parented their mules. Humiliated by the hatred toward pagan deities for centuries, exhausted by the burden of the plow and the heavy weight of the humans who rode her, she leads her children down the coastal road that borders the Mediterranean Sea. Trudging toward the ancient city of Ashkelon, the Biblical home of the Hebrew judge, Samson, and his Philistine wife, Delilah, she dreams she will find worshippers, earn rest, and finally know peace. But, by this time, she is a walking shadow, nothing more.

THE CONSPIRACIES OF DREAMS

Ishmael

TEL AVIV, ISRAEL

MAY 1979

I haven't thought about Danny O'Halloran in years. No, that's not exactly true. Danny is in the corner of my mind where I place memories I don't want to remember. But on this Friday afternoon, memories of Danny will obsess me. Although I don't know it now, in three minutes I will recall every detail of the last time I saw Danny. That was when I knew where my loyalties lay, when I knew whom I must love, when I knew what I had to do, when I knew my conscience was clear.

But at this moment Danny is far from my thoughts. I am impatiently sitting with two other diplomats in our Arab taxi which, with its green and white Palestinian license plate, is too conspicuously parked in front of a pizzeria on Levinsky Street. The cab driver and the other diplomats speak only Arabic which is why, since I speak Hebrew fluently, my government selected me to travel to the last place on earth I want to go. Our shrewd driver has stationed himself across from that Israeli gift to monstrously grotesque architecture, the Tel Aviv Central Bus Terminal, and continuously asks Arabs who are about to go into the terminal if they would like to ride in his air-conditioned cab to Gaza.

He beckons to a bearded man in a black caftan who is about to enter the station.

"Why take an Israeli bus which stops at every city and settlement between here and the border? Why not ride in comfort with Arabs to Gaza?"

The man peers through the cab window at us and declines. "I'm going north to Haifa. And even if I weren't, I wouldn't go with you. Why should I ride in a crowded taxi when I can sit in comfort in an air-conditioned bus which charges half as much as you do?"

Our cab driver shrugs his shoulders and tells the three of us who are anxious to leave Tel Aviv that gas is too expensive to drive all the way to Gaza with less than four fares. While the other two fume impatiently I am almost ready to get on a slow bus.

I am in Israel against my will. I have no desire to relive painful memories of my several espionage assignments here. But, since my mother was born in Jerusalem and I vacationed with her family in Palestine for many years, the Egyptian High Command decided I was the perfect diplomat to go to Tel Aviv to finalize details of the peace treaty Egypt will sign with Israel at the end of the month in Washington, D.C.

What a farce!

For several days my two colleagues and I engaged in delicate diplomatic calisthenics to regain the Sinai Peninsula that we lost in our last war with Israel. This barren moonscape of 61,000 square kilometers of sand and rocks was ours for centuries until the Ottoman Empire, and then the British, seized it from us. We Egyptians can always use a little more desert. And the Israelis will have one less hostile nation on its border.

President Sadat and I agree that if Egypt fights against Israel, both countries will suffer major losses; if we talk, we will both win. So, he will go to Camp David, sign the treaty, win the Nobel Prize for peace, and war between the Arabs and Jews will be postponed for another nanosecond.

My colleagues, in a foolish economical gesture, refused a limousine and a chauffeur for our ride back to Gaza where we will catch a ship that will take us to Cairo. Instead, without informing me, they picked a taxi whose driver turns out to be the cheapest, craftiest know-it-all in the entire Middle East. The other diplomats are anxious to leave Israel because they want to go home; but leaving Israel is uppermost on my mind because I am deluged by memories of betrayal and trust, of love and hate, of duty and reckless irresponsibility, of dreams deferred and dreams denied.

And then, because I am fortune's fool, I see her. After I read this morning's paper I thought I could. Not true. I prayed I would. My Rebecca, but not my Rebecca. She is running frantically through the crowd toward the bus terminal; her handbag swings wildly from her shoulder, her shoes pound an alarming "get out of my way" click-clack on the concrete sidewalk.

In her haste she bumps into a dark-haired little girl wearing a pink top. Blue and gold butterflies flit across the front of the shirt and one butterfly delicately sips nectar from a white lily on each sleeve. Her white shorts reveal little legs that should someday break men's hearts.

Walking beside the girl is a woman who is carrying a large shopping bag. Startled, she grabs the child to prevent her from falling. As she steadies her, the bag tips over, and tomatoes, onions, and cucumbers spill across the street. The mother shouts at Rebecca, "Watch where you're going! You almost knocked my daughter down."

I am surprised that Rebecca does not stop running and help the woman pick up her vegetables; she merely waves an apologetic hand at the couple and frantically cries, "Please, please excuse me; I must catch the noon bus to Ashkelon, I'm sorry," and she runs even faster toward the terminal.

While the mother simultaneously glares at Rebecca's back and stoops to pick up her bruised tomatoes, her daughter runs ahead of her into the restaurant. Instead of following her little girl into the pizzeria, the woman shades her eyes from the fierce noonday sun with her right hand and vengefully grins as she (and I) realize that no matter how desperately Rebecca runs the last few hundred feet she will never reach the sixth floor of the terminal in time to catch her bus.

While Arabs and Jews have a hostile and volatile history, they do agree on one detail. They both concur that the Tel Aviv Central Bus station is a more complex labyrinth than the one Daedalus constructed to house the Minotaur. Finding the platform from which one's bus is scheduled to depart requires the patience of Job and the skill of an Arctic explorer searching for the North Pole in a blizzard.

First, the harried passenger weaves through aisles where stores are anxiously going bankrupt. Next, confused and frustrated passengers grope through endless passageways which lead nowhere. Peace between Muslims and Jews will occur before anyone makes sense of the terminal's maze of convoluted corridors. Even if Rebecca masters the twists and turns of the station's architectural digressions she will never reach the platform in time. I silently plead with the god of bus drivers to somehow delay her and give me a chance to atone for what I did to her so many years ago.

Twenty-three years have passed since I first met Rebecca. Even though she is past forty, she is still slender, still graceful, still elegantly beautiful, still has silken black hair without a trace of silver. She is still exotically seductive. I still love her. Yet, I still dare not love her.

Suddenly Rebecca stops running toward the terminal. I stop dreaming about her. The mother screams. The crowds in the street stop shopping, arguing, cursing, walking, talking, bargaining, stealing, loving, hating. But the people inside the pizzeria do not stop. They explode toward my cab in one thunderous, fiery eruption. The little girl catapults into the air with the dozen or so other customers and falls with a sickening thud amid thousands of pieces of shattered bloody fragments of pizza, glass, arms, legs, ears, noses, intestines. All I hear now are the mother's terrified screams; all I think of now is Danny O'Halloran.

Ishmael

A Chance at Redemption

May 1979

"Two can keep a secret if one of them is dead" admonishes an old proverb. But the dead are not to be trusted. Secrets worm themselves out of the grave. And the living weave inextricable webs that are entangled in the inevitable challenges of life, its pleasures and disappointments, its remembered yesterdays and hoped-for tomorrows. Inevitably, the secret succumbs to the mercy of blind fate and decides to reveal itself and play havoc with the destiny of both the living and the dead.

Now, with death all around us, I run toward the living Rebecca. As sirens shriek and people scramble away from the smoldering pizzeria, I jump from the taxi. When I reach her, she is an animated scream of grief and has no idea who I am. How can she? In no way do I resemble the slim, handsome, keen-eyed, smooth-shaven 23-year-old, romantic Isaac Ben Abraham she once knew and loved. I'm sure she thinks I'm just a concerned European-suited Arab bystander who must wear glasses because my eyes, like the rest of me, are middle aged.

"Are you all right?" I ask her.

She does not answer me. Her gaze is transfixed on a little arm encased in a pink shirt sleeve that flutters gently in the breeze, which gives the illusion that the butterfly is still flying. I carefully put my arm around Rebecca's shoulders, almost cradling her. How often I have dreamed of doing this, but never under such circumstances.

Suddenly, she begins to tremble uncontrollably. She whispers hysterically to herself, "I knew I was going to miss the bus; I should have stopped and apologized to the mother. If I had helped her pick up her groceries, and told her how beautiful her little girl is, the child wouldn't have gone into that pizzeria before the bomb detonated. But I distracted the mother and now this."

"If you hadn't bumped into them, the mother would have gone with her child into the restaurant and they would both be dead."

"I'm sure the mother wants her daughter beside her, all the customers in the pizza parlor alive, and the terrorists who planned this attack blown up by their own bomb."

"Probably so."

Together she and I stare at the street filled with shards of broken glass, bits of bleeding human remnants, and panic-stricken onlookers. The nightmarish scene of incinerated bones and the smell of burning flesh assaults us. Rescue workers swarm out of an ambulance that is desperately wailing its two-toned siren. I'm amazed Rebecca doesn't find it odd that the one person comforting her is an Arab. She is in shock; hysteria is preventing her from realizing that. But then, she has never seen me as I really am. Love is as deceptive as hate.

"We should get out of here," I tell her. "Why were you in such a hurry to catch the bus?"

Reality suddenly hits Rebecca. She looks around in vain. "I must be in Ashkelon before the Sabbath, which begins at sundown. After this terrorist attack no other bus will run today." She gestures despairingly toward the horrific scene.

At that moment my cab driver yells at me to come back to the taxi. He no longer wants to wait for a fourth fare. I doubt if he will wait more than ten seconds for me. At this moment I realize that my delusional fantasy can become a reality. For years I have dreamed of revealing my identity to Rebecca. I no longer want to be a dead person who is keeping a secret. Fate in its most ironical way has given me my best chance to tell her all. I am tired of measuring out my life in secrets.

"Look, my taxi driver is taking us to Gaza where we will connect with a ship which will take us to Egypt. Ashkelon is on the way. He really wants a fourth fare. Why don't you come with us? That way his day will be profitable, and you'll get to Ashkelon before the Sabbath."

Rebecca seems to suddenly realize with whom she is speaking. She involuntarily shudders. I can see she thinks that it would be insane for an Israeli woman to get into an Arab cab with three Egyptian men.

"If you stay here, you will not be able to get to Ashkelon before the Sabbath. I know you think it is crazy to go with me, but look what all the sane people are doing! And I, Ishmael al Mohammed, guarantee your safety."

I don't wait for Rebecca to tell me what she thinks of my dubious guarantee, and shepherd her into the cab. Still shaking from the horrors she has witnessed, she doesn't resist. She enters the cab and sits in the middle of the backseat, I sidle in beside her, slam the door, and bark at the astounded cab driver in Arabic, "Let's go! You've got your fourth passenger."

Without hesitation he guns the accelerator and beeps his horn in imitation of the emergency sirens. None of the Israelis stop us as the taxi slowly edges through the crowd, turns the corner, and drives south. Before the taxi can enter the highway, we meet a roadblock. As the cab driver stiffens in fear, I hand the guards our diplomatic papers. I briefly explain the purpose of our mission in Israel, express our horror at the terrorist action, and state convincingly that it is an attempt to defeat the treaty. When the police cast a questioning eye at Rebecca, I quickly add that we are escorting an Israeli delegate back to her home in Ashkelon.

"She is very religious and must reach her house before her Sabbath. We consider it a friendly gesture to a diplomatic colleague since no bus will leave now."

Israelis are the least gullible of people and have the franchise for sniffing out any deception. As the guard looks questioningly at Rebecca, she smiles at him and emphatically looks at her watch. I note that she leans forward so he can see the beautiful Star of David necklace suspended from a gold chain around her neck.

"I must be home before sundown," she states firmly.

I am relieved when he hands us back our papers and lifts the barrier. We escape Tel Aviv's turmoil behind us and head south on Route 2 which hugs the coast of the Mediterranean Sea.

The very first time I saw Rebecca, I was struck by her magnificent eyebrows which emphasized her sad, sensitive eyes and her delicate nose. She reminded me of a mosaic tile portrait of the ancient Roman empress, Galla Placidia, that I had seen when I was on a mission in Ravenna, Italy. Galla was the wife of a pagan chieftain and the mother of a Byzantine emperor who championed Christianity at a time when it was dangerous to do so. She had such a sad, haunting gaze that I spent more time learning about this fascinating woman's history than I did in carrying out my mission, which was to talk a great deal and say nothing.

I fell in love with the long dead Galla Placidia as I stood before her pensive, poignant portrait in the Church of San Vitale. I felt that same emotion on the day I first saw Rebecca. I still feel the same way about her. Middle-aged men like me should leave romanticism and idealism to young fanatics. Otherwise, our old age is cursed. I am cursed.

Our trip to Ashkelon will take about an hour, maybe more, since traffic is Friday-afternoon heavy. I can see that Rebecca is beginning to feel extremely uneasy. I watch as she agitatedly clenches and unclenches her fingers. She realizes that soon we will leave the bumper to bumper traffic behind us and then the highway will narrow to a two-lane road surrounded by solitary fields and lonely beaches.

"Nervous, Rebecca?"

She does not respond, nor would any rational Israeli woman under similar circumstances. Terrorists have just blown up an Israeli pizzeria and slaughtered little children and housewives; she is probably thinking that we will be driving toward a deserted field where we will rape and kill her.

"How do you know my name?" she asks.

I am so nervous that I stare out of the car window at the Mediterranean for a few moments in order to calm myself. Then I reach into my inside breast pocket, take out my wallet, remove several well-worn pictures from it, and hand them to her.

"You have no reason to be concerned. I know you are Rebecca Neuwirth. I read in today's newspaper that your father, Aaron Silverman, the mayor of Ashkelon, fell and broke his leg yesterday. You live in Tel Aviv and work in a law office, but you wish you were an actress or a dancer. You have three children, a daughter and two sons; the oldest boy is a jet fighter pilot in the Israeli Air Force. You married Simon Neuwirth one month after the Suez War ended in 1956."

"How do you know all this about me? How do you know Aaron Silverman is my father? Who **are** you?"

I make no reply, but indicate with a brief nod that she should examine the photos. She holds them gingerly as though she is afraid not just to look at them, but even to touch them. She glances at the diplomat on her left and sees that he is sound asleep, snoring softly, with his mouth slightly open. The taxi driver, in a rapid-fire conversation with the diplomat who sits beside him in the front seat, is solving the entire Middle East problem to the amusement of his companion.

I light a cigarette and studiously ignore Rebecca as I continue to stare intently at the timeless sea. Slowly, tentatively, she looks at the first photo and gives a gasp as she stares at a picture of herself walking together with her parents, brothers, sister, aunt, and uncle in Ashkelon's town square when she must have been 19 years old. Her older brother is wearing the uniform of a lieutenant in Israel's elite military unit of paratroopers and her uncle is in the military full-dress uniform of an air force general.

"How did you get this picture? I've never seen it before. Who gave it to you?"

"Do you remember where you went with your family after your walk?"

"No."

"Try. What did you do that day?"

It is clear that Rebecca is making mental calculations as she tries to comprehend what is happening. Finally, after many seconds, she replies.

"It was so long ago. How do I know which day it was? I walked with my family every Saturday afternoon. It was a family tradition."

"But were your aunt and uncle with you every weekend?"

"No, only once a year, on their vacation."

She studies the picture closely. "David, my brother, was a lieutenant in the paratroopers in June, 1956, just before the Suez War. I was 19 then."

"What did you do for fun that summer?"

"For fun? I worked as a dance instructor and I was supposed to be in a play."

"Supposed to be?"

"The director was shot and killed by Arab terrorists during rehearsals. We cancelled the production."

She glares at me as though I represent every Arab terrorist in the world. I nod sympathetically and say, "I understand."

"I had hoped to go on the stage. I wanted to dance, sing, act, and be famous. You know how young girls dream."

"What happened to your dream?"

"Reality set in. Shortly after the war ended I married, had three children and fed my family. Dreams are a luxury I cannot afford."

She studies the picture for a few moments. "I am really intrigued. How did you get this picture?"

"I took it."

"You took it! When? Why?"

"When? The summer of '56. Why? Because I loved Egypt and because it was my job. But I keep it because I love you!"

Ishmael

THE ASSIGNMENT

ASHKELON, JUNE 1956

The Middle East has always been one of the most volatile areas in the world. But when Israel declared its independence, Egypt caused this tension to escalate and supported regular attacks on Israeli soil. Worse than the incursions by Egyptian fedayeen is that Nasser, the president of Egypt, blockaded the Straits of Tiran which prevented Israel from using the port of Eilat to gain access to the Red Sea. Nor does Egypt allow Israel to use the Suez Canal. Thus, Israel cannot trade with East Africa, India, China or Japan.

Egyptian intelligence is well aware in the summer of 1956 that Israel is contemplating an attack upon its hostile Arab neighbors and could probably advance toward the Straits of Tiran via the Sinai desert. Consequently, our Egyptian spies are infiltrating areas bordering the Sinai to observe signs of mobilization by the Israeli defense forces. Ancient Ashkelon, which the Israel army captured from the Arabs in 1948, lies only eight miles from Gaza. Therefore, this city is one of the prime targets of our undercover agents.

For several days, my captain, Omar Nafouz, and I have been sitting quietly in Ashkelon's sidewalk cafes and walking its streets while we unobtrusively observe the activities of its citizens. Intense, dark, handsome, chain-smoking, and Hebrew speaking, we blend in perfectly with the native population and attract no suspicion from the ever nervous, ever watchful, ever cautious Israelis.

All Israel is known to us. We have studied her mountains, deserts, valleys, rivers, and seas. We know she is the crossroad for every Christian, the star for every wandering Jew, the crescent moon shining for every Muslim. Her great, tortured capital, Jerusalem, which, ironically, means the "City of Peace," has seen more wars than possibly any other area in the world. Site of the Dome of the Rock, The Wailing Wall, the Church of the Holy Sepulcher, this city is sacred to the three great monotheistic creeds. But no people, no matter how hard they try, can possess her or Israel entirely and eternally, holy promises notwithstanding. Omar and I survey this sliver of barren sand which has inspired people to achieve the highest of ethical ideals and we scheme, as so many millions have before us, to capture this land of milk and honey, grape and olive, water and desert.

But how does anyone dwell peacefully in this country that is, and always has been, surrounded by nations that are united only by their hatred of her and their desire to possess her?

My father, General Ali al Mohammed, has groomed me to be perfectly suited for this espionage assignment in Israel. I speak Hebrew fluently because my mother was born in Jerusalem and is a member of the wealthy and influential Husseini clan. Not only is she a distant cousin of Jerusalem's Grand Mufti, Haj Amin el Husseini, she once proudly confided to me that her uncle, Dr. Musa Husseini, was one of the chief plotters responsible for the assassination of King Abdullah of Jordan. He and the other conspirators killed the king because he was about to sign a peace treaty with Israel. "We will never make peace with Israel, never! Any traitor who does so deserves to die," she frequently reminds me. Although her family has influential and patriotic Palestinian connections, my Egyptian-born father constantly stresses to me that every first-born son in our family has been a general in the Egyptian army since the time of the pharaohs.

Once I mischievously asked my father, "Were we called the al Osiris family then? Did we chase the Hebrew slaves to the Red Sea? Did we switch our name to al Zeus when the Greeks conquered

Egypt? When Mark Antony made love to Cleopatra, did we become the al Jupiters?"

"How dare you joke about your religion? Your duty? Your obligations? Your name?" my father exploded and stalked out of the room. He did not speak to me for three weeks. After that episode, both he and the holy imam of our mosque severely lectured me never again to ridicule Islam, Mohammed, or anything my father said.

My mother's family had fled from their luxurious home in Jerusalem when the United Nations created the Jewish state. They were sure that they would return within a week after my mother's cousin, General Abd el Kader el-Husseini, an idolized commander of the Palestinian army, defeated the ill-equipped Israeli armed soldiers who, in reality, were untrained pioneers.

But the general died during a fierce battle over Kastel Hill, an area six miles west of Jerusalem which was the beginning of the end of Palestinian hopes of conquering Israel. So my grandparents' dream of returning to their home in triumph became one of desperate longing familiar to every refugee whose memories idealize that which has been lost.

Their dream deferred became my dream referred.

My mother and grandparents taught me all they knew about Israeli culture. Also, I had spent a great deal of time in Jerusalem with the Husseinis until the war in 1948 made them refugees. They fled to Egypt and settled down near my father's ancestral home in Cairo. From an early age I knew my family, indeed my country, would depend on me to use my knowledge of Israel to restore all the land between the Jordan River and the Mediterranean Sea to Arab hegemony once again.

Of all the assignments I have had since I joined military intelligence this is the one I am sure will enable Palestinians to reestablish dominance in the land the Zionists now control.

While Omar and I sit and smoke at a small sidewalk cafe in the benign noonday sun we carefully observe a group of people, two of whom are men in Israeli military uniforms, walking and laughing as they approach a table near us.

We note that the older man is a brigadier general in the air force and one of the two young men behind him is a lieutenant in a paratroop unit.

Just then the teenage girls in the group stop abruptly to read a notice posted on a column beside a small theater next to the café's outdoor dining area.

"Look, a casting call," says the older of the two, a dark haired, tall, slim girl on the brink of becoming a very attractive woman.

"Why don't you try out, Rebecca?" asks one of the older women. "You were great in last year's play."

"But that was *Showboat*. This is a boring biblical story of Samson and Delilah. Who wants to be in that?" pouts the younger teen-ager, blonde and green-eyed, who bears no resemblance to the older, darker girl, although it's obvious by their familiar behavior toward each other that they are sisters.

The young lieutenant teases her, "Maybe they'll need some sexy dancing girls. They always have half-naked harem girls peeling grapes and swaying their hips in front of leering sheiks." He shakes his hips in a burlesque imitation of a belly dancer and hums a few notes from a seductive Arabic melody.

"Hey, David, you're pretty good," chuckles the general. "Maybe you should go with them."

"Seriously, Hannah," says the dark-haired girl, "maybe we should audition. Okay, it's not *Showboat*. But it's still a chance to be on the stage. It says here that tryouts are being held at one this afternoon for both actors and dancers. And everyone who shows up and doesn't get a major role can be part of the crowd in the temple and the special pagan worship dance that a choreographer has created especially for this production."

"Oh, I can just see Hannah dancing for the Philistines at the temple," jokes the lieutenant. He wiggles his hips seductively again while everyone, including the green-eyed girl, laughs uproariously.

"Really, Rebecca," she demands, "Do you want to be in one of those boring, stilted biblical plays that no one wants to see? Old people just come because the building is air-conditioned."

"And," groans the lieutenant, "relatives of the actors come because they're forced to, or their sisters will kill them."

"Look, acting is acting and an audience is an audience. If this is the play some director picked, then this is the play I'm going to audition for. If you can find a better offer in this cultural wasteland, take it." She stalks into the theater.

Hannah hesitates a moment, shrugs her shoulders, and reluctantly follows her older sister. Before she enters the building she turns and tells her brother, "We'll meet you at the café after the audition. Save some seats for us."

"Good luck" calls one of the older men. He resembles Rebecca so much that Omar and I gather he must be the dark-haired girl's father.

"Those girls must be relatives of the general," observes Omar. We watch the family approach the café and take a table near us. "And the lieutenant must be the girls' brother. Ishmael, try out for the play."

"What?"

"The way to meet the general and the lieutenant is through the girls."

"I don't want to be in an idiotic play with amateur Israelis who can't act," I protest.

"Weren't you in plays at Sandhurst, the Royal Military Academy in England? I heard you were a lousy Henry V, but a very passable Othello. Besides, all spies are actors. Join the cast. Get a part as an extra, a stagehand, anything. Then get very friendly with one of the sisters. Meet the family. Become one of them. Let the girl think you love her. The family will trust you and the rest will be easy."

I stare at Omar incredulously. "Easy? Pass myself off as a stage-struck Casanova of an Israeli! I fight Israelis; I don't make love to them. You're out of your mind."

Omar smiled. "It's a great cover."

"Spy, actor, lady's man. What a job description!"

"Yeah, it's really tough flirting with pretty girls. I heard you had an affair with every one of your leading ladies in England. And spying beats military maneuvers in the desert."

I slam my fist down hard on the table, but instead of retorting angrily, I light a cigarette and sit smoking silently for a long time. While I struggle to control my rage toward Omar, he continues to stare insistently at me. I deliberately avoid his gaze.

"Listen, Ishmael, I didn't want you for this assignment. The High Command made me take you because you speak Hebrew so fluently. I'd do the job myself if I didn't have such an obvious Egyptian accent. Ever since that incident in the desert all I thought you were fit for was to push a pencil somewhere in a basement so deep that a mole couldn't find you."

"If it were your brother..."

"Dammit! I'd still do my job. We've all lost relatives in wars. Now go inside the theater. Make one of those girls think she is the only girl you could ever love. Since you have a track record as a Casanova, that should be easy for you. Get me some information I can use, or I'll put you behind a desk myself. I don't care if your father is General al Mohammed. Act like a son of his.

"Do a damn good job when you read for a part, and tell everyone your name is Isaac Ben Abraham."

"Why that name?"

"The pretty girl is named Rebecca."

"So what?"

"Idiot, don't you know anything about the Jewish religion?"

Resignedly, I take a last puff from my cigarette, crush the stub in the ashtray, and self-consciously run my fingers through my hair. I slowly rise, walk toward the little theater and read the casting call posted on the pillar beside the door. I look back at Omar, who stares pointedly at me and then glances quickly at the general and the lieutenant who are sitting at one of the café's tables, totally oblivious of our existence. Squaring my shoulders, I resolutely enter the theater.

Abraham, the First Dreamer

BEERSHEBA, THE LAND OF CANAAN

CIRCA 1800 B.C.E.

They are laughing as I lie dying. Someone has left the tent flap open, and the hot, dusty breeze swirling around my bedroll only makes me feel worse. Outside, my eight sons are gathered around one of my wells with my second wife, Keturah. They've waited a long time for me to exit this world. Many, many years from now a book called Genesis will be written about me that will state with great authority that I was 175 when I died. I should only live so long. I listen to their idle chatter and I note how different the joking and convivial chatter among Keturah's six sons is from the hostile bickering between my two oldest boys, Isaac and Ishmael.

I came here to Shechem, near Beersheba, from Ur, the great city between the Tigris and Euphrates Rivers on the Persian Gulf. My family and I lived there until the Akkadians attacked us. Along with Sarah, my first wife, my father Terah, an idol maker, and my nephew Lot and his wife, I fled from Ur to Syria to escape those genocidal fanatics who wanted our beautiful land.

My father hated to give up his workshop. He was particularly good at making idols of his favorite goddess, Palés, the donkey deity who protected the flocks and made women fertile. Once, as a young child, I was playing in his shop and accidentally broke a clay idol of her he had just taken out of his kiln.

My father looked at me sadly as he bent down to pick up the fragile fragments of clay. "Now Palés will curse you, and your wife will be childless or bear children with great difficulty. If you do have children, they will curse each other from generation to generation. Pray to the goddess. Ask her to forgive you."

I looked at the broken fragments in his hands and tried to keep from laughing. "Papa, what's the use in praying to a goddess or god that you can form from clay and I can break? I believe in a God that creates us; not in one you make out of clay."

"King Gilgamesh's wife asked me to make this idol for her. The queen is desperate since he beats her every month because she does not become pregnant. She will pay more for this one idol than I have earned all year making idols for commoners."

"If Gilgamesh spent less time chasing after monsters with his friend Enkidu and more time with her, she might have a baby," I said with a smirk.

"Maybe if I make the idol for her out of gold instead of clay, you won't be able to break it. I don't care if she has a son or not. I have to make a living. Your god forbids idol worship? That kind of religion won't make us wealthy," my father said as he selected a new mold.

What does he worship then? I wondered. *Money or Palés?*

A week later I walked into his shop and grudgingly had to admire the exquisite gold donkey idol he had created for Gilgamesh's queen. Suddenly I heard three ear-blasting roars from his shofar, a trumpet he had made from a ram's horn.

"Everyone get on the donkeys. We must leave now!" he bellowed at the top of his voice from the front of our tent, as my wife scrambled to gather as many of her precious possessions as she could.

"What's the matter? Why are you so upset?" asked my nephew Lot as he ran out of his nearby tent.

"The Akkadians are coming. Instead of protecting us, Gilgamesh is in the Cedar Forest with Enkidu hunting a monster he calls the Humbaba. I don't give a damn if he kills the Humbaba, but I don't want the Akkadians to kill us. Get on those donkeys!"

"Where can we go?" Lot asked in a panic. He is useless. I can see I will always have to watch over him.

"I have cousins in Syria; we can go there," Sarah proposed.

We fled so quickly that my father did not take any of his idols with us. In fact, we only took enough water and food for a few days, and very little clothing, because we knew the ruthless Akkadian army, who believed in the scorched-earth policy of warfare, was quickly advancing toward Ur. After we traveled for a few miles he remembered that he had left the beautiful golden statue of Palés in his shop. Since we did not dare go back for it, the Akkadians seized it and took it back with them to Nineveh, along with all the other treasures they stole from our homeland. In 1884 an Englishman will find it and take it to the British Museum. Imagine! My father's idol will be in one of the greatest museums of the world, and he will never receive a penny for all his hard work. The Lord works in mysterious ways.

We lived in Syria for 17 years until my father could bear his exile from Ur no longer and he went to live with his gods. Then the rest of us came here to the land of Canaan, and settled north of the Negev Desert. Although I scorned my father's belief in the power of Palés, my wife, Sarah, was barren, my flocks were lean, and their wool was stringy.

My God, the one true God, *Adonai Elohenu*, not the gold, silver, and clay idols that the rest of the world worships, told me in a dream that Canaan is the land He promised to me and my descendants, who would be as many as the stars.

Some Promise! Some Dream!

While my God promises me many descendants, Sarah cannot become pregnant. And Canaan, the land where He told me to go, while beautiful, has summer droughts, winter torrents, hordes of locusts that devour the crops, and a dead sea filled only with fantastic salt obelisks carved by the desert winds. Later, Lot's unfortunate wife will become one of these salt obelisks when she dares to look back at Sodom as her home is destroyed.

This land transforms all who love it.

We were here only a short time when a terrible famine swept the parched country. My sheep died of thirst, our crops withered, and Sarah was still as barren as the soil I have grown to love. I had two choices: starve or go to Egypt.

Sarah was very beautiful and I knew the princes of Egypt would tell Pharaoh that a lovely foreigner was seeking food and refuge in his country. I knew he would take her into his harem and would have no compunction doing away with me, a mere marital obstacle.

Therefore, I invented a lie to protect the truth.

"Tell them you are my sister; if Pharaoh thinks I am your brother he will not only let me live, but even reward me for letting you go to him," I counseled her.

And compensate me he did. Sarah was so gorgeous that he gave me many sheep, oxen, camels, donkeys, and servants as a bride-price. Of course, when he saw how often the two of us met and how we behaved toward each other, he realized that she was my wife. To my astonishment and immense relief, he did not execute me. He now was my friend, and he loved Sarah. When he understood that I had to lie to save my life he knew that something was rotten in the state of Egypt. It is not often that immorality sickens a pharaoh and his court.

Therefore, he permitted Sarah and me to return to our home with all the possessions he had given us. My wife was fond of one servant in particular, Hagar, a lovely, high-cheeked, sloe-eyed, slim woman with wide hips made for childbearing.

I was not too jealous when Sarah went to Pharaoh; I don't understand why my wife reacted so vehemently when she discovered that Hagar was going to have my baby. After all, she was the one who reluctantly told me to try to have a child with Hagar since she could not conceive; who am I to refuse such an offer?

When Hagar became pregnant the first night I slept with her, she bragged incessantly. This made my childless wife feel desperate and she made life miserable for Hagar. Finally, the Egyptian girl couldn't take Sarah's harassment anymore, and she fled into the

Negev desert. But I knew that Hagar, even if she were not pregnant, could never survive in that scorching, desolate place. I secretly sent a servant to convince the mother of my soon-to-be-born child to return. The servant told her that the baby would be a boy who would become a mighty giant and run wild like the desert donkeys in the Negev. And so I became the father of a son from that sweet, long-suffering, and beautiful Egyptian.

I named him Ishmael, which means "God heard me," and he became a strong archer who showed great promise. I made the two women agree to live together, but such a tense, hostile atmosphere filled the tent that I ran off to fight against four kings to gain some peace.

Finally, Sarah had a son and she was wild with joy. She laughed and fussed over him all the time. She even named him Isaac to symbolize how much laughter he brought to her in her old age. I must admit it is hilarious to think she had a child when she was 90. Now, the Good Book says she was 90, but women always lie about their age. Sarah was not only bad at figuring out dates; she was horrible at math as well. But I have learned that not only must a husband never forget his wife's birthday, he must also never ask her how old she is.

Isaac's birth made her relationship with Hagar even more acrimonious. Sarah was determined that even though Ishmael was my firstborn, he should be completely disinherited. She wanted her son, and only her son, to inherit my wealth, my prestige, and my land.

The mothers fought constantly and influenced how the boys felt about each other. Finally, I decided to take my two sons away on a three-day trip so we could enjoy one another's company, roast a ram over a campfire, and give thanks to God that we finally had some peace without the jealous women around.

As I gazed at my children contentedly chewing on the rack of lamb, I could see the Egyptian features Ishmael had inherited from his mother in his almond–shaped eyes, his high cheekbones, and his assertive nature.

But Isaac is my Ur-Child. He has all the characteristics of my people. His trusting nature and simple, goodhearted, gentle ways endear him to me. He has my father's artistic talent, and he resembles Sarah. I adore Isaac. My God has overpowered Palés' curse.

When we came home, Hagar was sure I had taken Ishmael on the trip to sacrifice him to Allah. At least, that's what the Koran, which won't be written for another two thousand years or so, will state. With the utmost difficulty I convinced her that I would never kill a child of mine, even though he is only the child of a servant.

Sarah, however, was certain that I had wanted to sacrifice Isaac to the Lord, my God, and she sank into a deep depression from which she never recovered. She was so inconsolable I promised her that our one true God, unlike the deities the savage pagans in this region worship, forbids human sacrifice. Then I told her that I would find a wife for Isaac from one of her relatives' children. She had heard that our cousin Bethuel had a beautiful daughter named Rebecca, and I promised her that I would arrange a marriage between Isaac and the young girl. This eased Sarah's heartache slightly.

Yet, when Ishmael was 13, Sarah forced me to send Hagar and the boy away. Sadly, I watched them disappear into the depths of the Negev Desert. Without Sarah's knowledge I sent a man after them to guide them to a well where they would be able to survive during the hot summer months. Later, Hagar found an Egyptian wife for Ishmael and he became the father of 12 sons who founded 12 tribes. Now, he is outside my tent waiting to bury me. What will he think as he shovels the dirt into my grave together with Isaac? What will become of my two sons who were destined from birth to compete with each other for my land and my God?

> Now they are men who will love to hate each other.
> Why **does** this land transform all who love it?
> Why can this land resurrect or shatter hearts?
> My God, my God, what did you promise me and my
> descendants?

Sarah's Fulfillment

THE LAND OF CANAAN

CIRCA 1786 B.C.E

I laugh with utter and complete joy. Thank you, God, for my son, my wonderful son. I laughed when I found I was with child. Then everyone laughed at me when Abraham proclaimed that I, an old gray-haired woman, became pregnant.

No one laughs because Abraham is bald and his beard is white.

Why do men lose the hair on their heads, but never on their faces? Abraham would look much better if he had hair on his shiny dome instead of on his cheeks and chin. The balder he becomes and the longer and whiter his beard grows, the more respect he commands.

The older and grayer I become, the less attractive I am to him.

And why can old men have children, but women must bear sons while they are young? And no woman is fulfilled until she has borne her husband a son. Now, I, an old woman, am fulfilled. Abraham even named my son Isaac which means "she laughed."

Only one person makes me stop laughing: Ishmael. I constantly see Hagar proudly praising every little accomplishment of his. She boasts that he will grow up to be a wild ass of a man, a powerful hunter. How could I have allowed Abraham to have a child with an Egyptian? Why did I think I was barren? How could I have been so mistaken?

Even though Abraham held a great feast when Isaac was weaned, I know how much my husband loves my slave's child. Ishmael must not inherit my son's rightful destiny and Abraham's land and wealth. Isaac will be the father of a son who will sire many sons, and a great nation shall descend from my twelve grandchildren. We will be a nation chosen by God and my son will be one of the great forefathers of this nation. And Isaac's child, Jacob, will even dream of wrestling with angels to see our God.

I curse Ishmael and all his descendants.

Hagar's Prophecy

THE LAND OF CANAAN

CIRCA 1773 B.C.E.

Sarah laughs! Her laugh poisons my heart and my hopes. She laughs at the loss of my child's dreams and at the fulfillment of hers. She has just born a son and her triumph is my tragedy, mine and my son, Ishmael's. She will name her child Isaac. In her language his name means "laughter," but this name will mean sorrow for my child.

Sarah never forgave me for giving birth to Abraham's firstborn, for giving him an heir. She despises the fact that I am prettier and younger than she is, more fertile than she is, and that I know how to cook, clean, and weave much better than she ever will. I know the time will come when she will force Abraham to drive Ishmael and me away. She will never allow my son to inherit his father's name and wealth.

But I will teach Ishmael well. I will find him an Egyptian wife, and he will become the father of 12 princes of 12 great nations. I will never let him forget that he was Abraham's first born. He will wander in the desert as a child of a maidservant, but he will seek his true destiny as Ishmael: the man who listens to God.

He will torment Isaac's descendants forever!

Ishmael

JERUSALEM

APRIL 1948

I hear the angel Israfil blowing his trumpet. It is the end of the world.

"Ishmael and Abdul, we're going this minute. *Get in the car now!*"

My father blasts the horn on his Mercedes three more times. Each trumpet howl contains more staccato-like urgency. He yells at my brother and me again to hurry.

"Do you want the Israelis to kill you?" he shouts, but invisible hands hold me back. My grandparents' house, the only home my mother knew until she married my father, is my small haven of warmth, love, and wonderful memories. This is the place where we always celebrated Eid al-Fitr, the three-day festival at the end of the holy month of Ramadan. Grandmother decorated the house with festive candles, crescent moons, and five pointed stars. We stuffed ourselves with rice dishes, dates, almonds, murgh mussallam, tabuli, nawabi biryam and lamb stew.

And the desserts were masterpieces. I can still taste her sheer korma, a spicy raisin pudding, and her pink cylindrical cakes covered with nuts which were the envy of every other baker in the entire universe.

There is the crack I made in the ceramic tile in the dining room when I dropped a pot on the floor. Grandfather never had time to mend the hole Abdul made in our bedroom window when he threw a ball at me so hard that instead of catching it I ducked. We both watched it sail out into the street, taking a shard of glass and our parents' wrath with it.

I love this house. I love this street. I love Jerusalem. I have great friends here whom I like better than the friends I have in Cairo.

But yesterday we attended the funeral of our cousin, General Abad El Kadar Husseini. A damned Israeli killed him after he conquered Kastel, a small village that guards the road to Jerusalem. The enemy sniper shot him after he gained control of the village and came back the next day for a tour of inspection. "Nothing like snatching defeat from the jaws of victory" goes the old cliché.

Thirty thousand mourners filled the Haram al Sharif, the Noble Sanctuary between the Dome of the Rock and the Al-Aqsa Mosque in the heart of Jerusalem, to honor Jerusalem's greatest hero. His funeral was in the same place where the prophet Mohammed ascended to heaven.

The Israelis have won Kastel. Now they are on the outskirts of Jerusalem, about to occupy our part of the city, our street, our grandparents' house, but they will never conquer our Dome of the Rock; they will never conquer my Jerusalem of Gold.

Abdul and I slide into the car, which is filled with our belongings and our memories. "Momma, I will get your house back for you someday. You'll see. I will do it for you, for Grandma and Grandpa, and especially for Cousin Husseini. The Israelis will live to regret that they killed him."

Call Me Isaac

In the Theater

June 1956

"Name, please?" asked a young red haired man sitting at a desk on a bare stage.

"Isaac Ben Abraham."

"Previous acting experience?"

"A little Shakespeare at college in England. I acted in a few plays."

"I'm an Oxford man myself. Did you go there?"

"No, I went to Sandhurst, the Royal Military Academy in Surrey. And I thought Milton's *Samson Agonistes* was a dramatic poem; I didn't know it could be performed."

"It was once on the radio. We're going to do the first live production. Sit over there and study this audition speech while I finish interviewing the rest of the applicants." The casting director hands me a script of *A Streetcar Named Desire*.

I think to myself, *What irony! To get the role of Samson, I have to become Stanley Kowalski?*

I sit down and begin to think how many nuances I can give to the line; "You and me had this date from the beginning, baby."

"Next. Name, please?"

"Rebecca Silverman," I hear the tall, dark-haired, very beautiful girl say.

"Previous acting experience?"

"I was Miss Julie in last year's production of *Showboat*."

"Ah, yes. I saw you," says the director's casting assistant. "You were very moving. And you're a good singer and an excellent dancer. That was a wonderful shuffle you did to "Can't Help Lovin' That Man of Mine." My daughters were imitating you for weeks. But this play is a drama which revolves around Delilah's treachery toward Samson."

"I thought it would revolve around Samson's strength," says Rebecca.

"In a way, it does," interjects Danny O'Halloran, the earnest young American director. "Delilah's treachery turns his moral weakness into spiritual strength. You have to make the audience sense that. Here, study this audition speech."

He hands her another script of *A Streetcar Named Desire*. Rebecca takes it and sits down to study the speech he indicates.

"Name, please?"

"Hannah Silverman," says the pretty reddish-blonde girl.

"You must be Rebecca's little sister."

"No, I'm her younger sister. I'm almost as tall as she is, so I can't be her little sister."

"Temperamental, aren't you? And what experience do you have?"

"I was Kate in *The Taming of the Shrew* and Parthy Hawks, Captain Andy's feisty wife, in *Showboat*.

"Typecasting, I see. Can you sing and dance as well as be temperamental?" the director said with a sarcastic smile.

"I thought this play was a drama."

"It is. But we'll need some dancing girls for the big temple scene."

"Shit."

"Keep that temper up and you'll steal the show."

Hannah grins, "Well, I won't like the part, but if you put the spotlight on me during my number, I'll show Samson how to bring the house down."

"Oh, God. A comedienne, yet. This is going to be a long summer."

"You mean I got the part? I'm underwhelmed." Hannah seductively belly dances over to her sister and sits down in disgust. Rebecca is studying her speech so intently that she barely notices how annoyed her sister is.

I watch the verbal banter with amusement. I have already decided that Hannah is the more skeptical and aggressive of the two sisters, and will be harder to get to know. The older girl, Rebecca, has a very sweet, gentle nature. She reminds me of an exotic mosaic painting I once saw in Italy of a fascinating empress. I have never talked to an Israeli woman before, and suddenly I nervously realize that this is the first time I have ever been the only Arab in a room filled entirely with Jews. I begin to perspire profusely, yet I sit next to the girls.

A young, very good looking Israeli sits down beside me and says, "Hi, I'm Simon."

"I'm Isaac."

He nods at the younger girl and says, "Watch out for Hannah. She's hotheaded, impulsive, and always gets her way. She's a sabra with more nerve than sense."

"Isn't her sister one too?"

"No, Rebecca came here with her family from Poland together with ours. Hannah was born here after her family settled in Ashkelon. So she's the one with chutzpah."

Hannah looks at us and winks, "When you get to know me, Isaac, you'll find I'm just like that Sabra pear, prickly on the outside and sweet on the inside."

"Really?" teases Simon. "You keep that sweet side hidden."

"You, of all people, Simon, will never see my sweet side."

"Why Hannah, I've already seen it and tasted it, too. It's most delicious."

Hannah glares at him, and then bursts out laughing. The two of them get up, and giggling together, drift over to the other side of the room to join the other young people who are waiting to audition. When Rebecca sees that I am alone, she sits down beside me.

"Is anyone else in your family interested in acting besides Hannah?" I ask Rebecca. I don't think this direct question will arouse any suspicions, and I hope it will lead the girl to talk about her relatives who are in the military.

"No, just Hannah and I love to act on the stage. My brother is much too shy to get up in front of an audience unless it's his paratroop unit. Simon, Hannah's friend, doesn't love to act. He just loves to tease Hannah."

"Did you and Hannah get the acting bug from your parents?"

"Heavens, no! My mom is the typical housewife, and my dad is always thinking of his business and politics. Last year he almost missed seeing us in *Showboat* because he was in the midst of a huge financial deal."

"So, only your older brother is in the military?"

"Hannah will begin basic training when she graduates from high school. I start mine in the fall, but after I finish my military service I'm going to study to be a dancer and an actress.

"But don't think the rest of the men in our family are not interested in defending Israel. One of our cousins is a jet fighter pilot, and my uncle is a brigadier general in the air force. Hannah and I will probably go into an army medical unit because girls aren't allowed in the paratroop fighting units. Men are so chauvinistic. They think we can't parachute from a plane into battle."

I silently marvel. I cannot imagine any well-brought-up Arab girl who would want to fight in the army. In fact, no Egyptian upper-class girl would be allowed to act on the stage. When I was in England it took me a long time to get used to seeing women walking in the streets without male escorts. To see British girls from upper and middle class families such as Vivien Leigh, Rachel Kempson, and Greer Garson become actresses and be admired by all was overwhelming. Here, Israeli women have even more equality than their English counterparts, if fighting in an army is a right women enjoy having.

I don't think, however, that any Israeli girl can act as well as an English one. All the English girls I have met seemed to be able to speak Shakespearean soliloquies eloquently from birth and intimidated me with their stagecraft. But then, attending Sandhurst did not give me many opportunities to socialize with many girls except the ones I met in the four Shakespearean productions in which I acted. Since my parents have already arranged a marriage for me with the daughter of close friends of theirs whom I like, but I will never love, I take any opportunity I can to have an affair with every pretty girl I meet.

As I look at Rebecca, who is transforming herself into Blanche DuBois, I am struck by the vast differences between my sheltered fiancée, the daughter of one of my father's friends, and this sweet, gentle actress who will soon be a soldier. Nor does she resemble the accomplished British girls who can play Desdemona one night and Cleopatra the next. I glance briefly at my own speech; when the director asks me to read, I do my very best Marlon Brando imitation.

I note that when it is Rebecca's turn to audition she does not try to mimic Vivien Leigh. Instead, she gives a very sensitive and original rendition of one of Blanche DuBois' heart wrenching speeches, and I find myself moved by her performance. Three other girls are also auditioning. After listening to them read, it's obvious to me that Rebecca is, by far, the most polished performer in the auditorium.

All of the other young men who read are terrible. I realize that I will be awarded the role of Samson, not because I am a born actor, but because the others are incredible amateurs.

After everyone finishes auditioning I sit beside Rebecca, but do not know how to renew the discussion about her brother and uncle. Yet, I reason that if we're both in the play, I'll have plenty of time to ask her seemingly innocent questions about them.

Much to my surprise, Rebecca initiates the conversation. "How did you happen to go to college in England?" she asks.

"My father is a professor of mathematics at Sandhurst Royal Military Academy in Surrey. My mother also teaches at the high school there. I came back to Israel to do my military service."

I hope she believes my extremely hollow lie. For a moment I consider telling her the truth which is that every male member of my family for several generations attended Sandhurst and then became an officer in the army. Naturally, I could not tell her that it was the Egyptian army in which my family served. Suddenly I'm relieved that I lied because, of course, Israel has only had an army for eight years. I must invent lies to protect the truth.

At that moment the director calls everyone to attention and announces who has won which part. As I surmised, Rebecca is cast as Delilah, and I am chosen to play the role of Samson. Simon is selected to be Manoah, Samson's father, and everyone else is given minor parts. While the entire cast congratulates Rebecca enthusiastically, I receive only a polite handshake from the director, for which I am grateful. I am extremely nervous about infiltrating Israeli society in such an intimate way, and I find it quite difficult to pretend to be friends with people who are my deadly enemies. It is excruciating to make people I hate like me. I take the practice schedule from a table on the stage, tell the director I will be on time for the first rehearsal, remember to smile warmly at Rebecca and quickly leave the auditorium.

As I walk toward the café to meet Omar, I chuckle to myself at the irony of the afternoon's events. I, Ishmael al Mohammed, have become Isaac Ben Abraham in order to discover when the Israeli military will mobilize and where it will attack Egypt. I will pretend to love an Israeli girl to foster Egyptian military supremacy. I will portray Samson, the Hebrew strongman who devastated the Philistines of Gaza and destroyed their great temple to enable Egypt to vanquish Israel's army and regain all the land from the Jordan River to the Mediterranean Sea. Like Delilah, who betrayed Samson, I will use treachery to defeat Rebecca and her people.

I walk toward Omar and slap the script down in front of him.

He lifts his glass in a toast. "The charade begins!"

Danny O' Halloran
First Rehearsal

June 1956

"Everybody on stage. I want to take a cast picture before we begin our first rehearsal. Tall guys in the back. Pretty girls in front. Come on, Hannah, smile. Pretend to be happy."

"Can't we do a modern musical comedy, Danny? How about *Oklahoma? Samson and Delilah* is such an old, boring, and absolutely untrue story. No man loses his strength because he cuts his hair, nobody can pull up huge trees with his bare hands, or kill a lion with the jawbone of an ass. And how could anyone catch 300 foxes and tie flaming torches to their tails and drive them through fields? Can you imagine a fox letting you do that to it? It would bite and scratch you if you did manage to catch it. It would be hard enough to catch one, let alone 300. Why are we doing this ridiculous play?"

"It's a pleasure to have such a religious, respectful cast member."

"Better than a gullible marshmallow. I was not born to be in a chorus of dancing slave girls. Do you know what magnificent talent you are letting go to waste?"

"I know, I know. You are big. It's the role that's small. Are you ready for your close-up now, or will you condescend to be part of the cast picture?"

"Really, listen. I would be perfect for the part of Ado Annie in *Oklahoma*."

To my amazement she begins to sing:

> "I'm just a girl who can't say no,
> I'm in a terrible fix,

I always say, 'come on, let's go,'
Just when I ought to say 'nix.'
When a person tries to kiss a girl,
I know she ought to give his face a smack
But as soon as someone kisses me
I somehow, sorta, want to kiss him back!"

And then she has the nerve to take a bow as the rest of the cast applauds her.

I have to admit she is a pretty good singer and actress. I love her grin and her moxie, or since I am in Israel, I guess I should say her *"chutzpah."*

Simon must be her boyfriend since he immediately puts his arm around her and gives her a kiss. "Isn't she marvelous?" he asks as he smiles proudly at Hannah.

"She's fabulous. Now let's take the cast picture."

As the cast takes their places I notice that Isaac looks uncomfortable, and I assume that he feels like an outsider. He didn't seem to know any of the other cast members and doesn't talk to anyone except Rebecca. Who can blame him? She is absolutely gorgeous. If I weren't engaged, I could fall in love with her. She is so different from Hannah that it is hard to believe they are sisters.

I take two photos of the assembled actors and promise, "I'll have these developed before opening night and give everyone a copy. Also, I'll have a big publicity poster for the play printed containing this photo and all your names, and I'll place it by the front door of the theater. You never know, Hannah, a famous Hollywood producer may see it and you'll become a great movie star."

"Danny, why are you always picking on me?"

"Because you're a girl who can't say yes."

"Now, places, everyone. Isaac, let's run through scene 6."

I'm curious to see what kind of reading the boy will give. I was reluctant to select him for the part, but he read his lines better than anyone else who auditioned.

He stands up, clears his throat, nervously runs his fingers through his hair, and begins:

> O glorious strength
> Put to the labor of a beast
> Debased lower than a bondslave!
> Promise was that I should Israel
> From Philistine yoke deliver
> Ask for this great Deliverer now
> And find him Eyeless in Gaza
> At the Mill with slaves
> Himself in bonds under Philistine yoke:
> Yet stay, let me not rashly
> Call in doubt divine prediction:
> What if all foretold had been fulfilled
> But through mine own fault.
> Who have I to complain of but myself?

"Isaac, that was one of the worst readings I have ever had the privilege of hearing. Come on, what's going through the character's mind when he says these lines?"

"He's upset because, despite his glorious strength, he's forced to work like a beast, like a slave in Gaza."

"Isn't the line 'eyeless in Gaza' famous?" asks Rebecca.

"Usually, cast," I explain, trying not to sound pedantic, "if a character in a play or novel is physically blind, the writer wants the audience to think this person has a powerful inner vision. Maybe, Isaac, you could manage to convey that idea. What do you think Samson is now able to see when he is eyeless in Gaza that he couldn't see when he had his sight?"

"That perhaps what happened to him was a 'divine prediction'?" ventures Hannah.

"No, no, no!" says Isaac. "Look at the last line of the speech. He says everything happened 'through my own fault.' A few lines further down he says he was 'weak in mind, in body strong.' It looks as though he's taking responsibility for his own actions and admitting he made some mistakes, instead of saying all his actions were divinely ordained."

"But," I interject, "everyone believes that it was Delilah, his wife, who betrayed him and enabled the Philistines to capture him. They think it was her fault, not Samson's, that he became eyeless in Gaza. Let's hear your speech, Delilah."

Rebecca stands up and eloquently recites to the admiration of the entire cast:

> The princes of my country came in person,
> solicited, commanded,
> Threatened, urged, adjured by all
> The bonds of civil duty and of
> Religion, pressed how just it was,
> How honorable, how glorious to
> entrap a common enemy who had
> destroyed such numbers of our nation.
> And the priest was ever at
> My ear preaching how meritorious
> With the Gods it would be to
> Ensnare an irreligious dishonorer
> Of Dagon. What had I to oppose
> Against such powerful arguments?
> Only my love of thee held long
> Debate and combated in silence all
> These reasons with hard contest.
> At length, I realized that to the public good
> private respects must yield.

"So, what she realizes is that her loyalty to her country and her religion are more important to her than her love for her husband," says Isaac.

"None of this would have happened," declares Hannah firmly, "if Samson had married a Hebrew woman instead of a person from Gaza."

"But," says Rebecca, "Delilah was Samson's wife. In his next speech Samson says that he chose her from among his enemies, loved her and told her all his secrets because he was so overpowered by his feelings for her. Once she became his wife, she was to leave her parents and her country, worship his God, not her Dagon, and be loyal to him and only him."

"Do you really think it's possible for a person to forget his homeland and forsake the religion of his people?" asks Isaac.

As most of the cast shake their heads I ask, "Can't you think of anyone who did?"

"Yeah, I can." says Simon. "Ruth, the grandmother of King David, did. After her husband died she told her mother-in-law, Naomi, 'Don't ask me to leave you and go back to my own people. Your people shall be my people and your God shall be my God.'"

"But her people weren't at war with Naomi's people," observes Isaac. "Doesn't that make a difference?"

"Does war have such an effect on love and loyalty?" I ask my cast. "To whom do lovers owe allegiance? To each other? To their families? To their countries? To their religion? Why I wanted to do this play instead of some cutesy musical, Hannah, is to explore what happens when either a lover or a country feels betrayed. What were Samson and Delilah's feelings about love and loyalty? Has anything changed in the last 3,000 years or are lovers from different countries still facing the same conflicts?"

I look expectantly at my cast. Isaac gazes blankly out the window and avoids looking at me. He is a strange person. Hannah pouts, but Rebecca gazes at me thoughtfully.

"All right, everyone. Let's take a break at the café next door. Then we'll come back and see if we can't convey some of these ideas to our audience, who, I hope to God, will be more than a few of our relatives. How are the ticket sales going?"

"My mom bought 20 tickets. Of course, she bought them for all our relatives," says Simon.

Everyone laughs. "Don't worry, Danny," Hannah smiles, "If it's a hot night, we'll sell out. We're one of the few places in town that has air conditioning."

"I hope so. Let's take a break and go across the street to the café for some cold drinks."

As the cast slowly leaves the auditorium, Rebecca and Isaac linger behind. I hear her ask Isaac, "Does this play demonstrate that conflicts never change and humans fight the same battles over and over again? Aren't any clashes ever resolved? Is the world nothing but a vicious circle that centers continually on the territorial and the religious imperative?"

My God, I think, *the girl has a brain*. I turn to Isaac. "What's your opinion?"

The young man shrugs his shoulders, turns his back on us, and walks quickly down the aisle and exits. Rebecca and I look at each other. I am amazed at Isaac's reaction and I can see she is, as well. She does not say anything to me, nor will I make a derogatory remark about one cast member to another. We slowly follow him.

Isaac is some leading man. Why in Hell did I pick him for the part of Samson? Maybe I should do Oklahoma.

Omar
THE WARNING
JUNE 1956

To my amazement the cast is walking out of the theater after only a half hour rehearsal. They're coming to the café in two's and three's except for Ishmael who looks upset and straggles after the rest of the cast in solitary gloom. None of them notices that I beckon to him with a slight nod before he follows them into the restaurant. He slouches moodily beside me at one of the outdoor tables in the shade under a huge palm tree. I glance cautiously around and see that no one is watching us. In fact, every other table is empty due to the afternoon heat. Air conditioning has come to Israel.

"Why is the rehearsal over so early?"

"We're just taking a break. That damned pedantic director is disgusted with my acting ability. He wants a method actor. Care to send me to the Actor's Studio in New York? I hear it's run by a Jew. Maybe he can teach me how to act like one.

"And that girl, Rebecca, wants to discuss political philosophy with me solely to impress me with her intelligence. She just asked me what I think about – *are you ready for this?* 'the cyclical nature of human conflicts.'"

"Good!" I say sarcastically.

"What's good about that?"

"She's trying to impress you. That means she's interested in you. If she's interested, she'll talk. Ask her about her brother and uncle. Also, that man who's playing Manoah?"

"Simon Neuwirth. What about him?"

"He's also a paratrooper. He's not in uniform because he's on a three-week furlough. Become friends with him."

"The director thinks I'm a dumb ass."

"The director has brains."

"I don't need any of your shit."

"You'll get plenty of shit from me if you don't get some valuable information. This place is ready to explode. I sit here and watch nervous Zionists who smoke cigarettes, drink coffee, and talk war non-stop. I see more and more men and women in military uniforms hitchhiking to military bases. I can smell an invasion coming. I want to know when and where.

"Now get in that restaurant. Sit down next to that gorgeous girl and charm her. With your good looks and your track record as a Casanova that should be easy for you. Tell her some sob story about yourself. Next, ask her to confide in you. Girls love that. Then go back and give the director the best reading he's ever heard."

Ishmael glares at me for a long, long moment before he gets up and lets the pavement take him into the café.

He's the worst agent I've ever had.

Rebecca

REVERIE

JUNE 1956

*W*hy *are handsome, charismatic, actors totally incapable of holding a serious conversation unless they're reading the words from a script? And Isaac can't even read his lines well. Not that I blame him. Who wants to be in a play that was written to be read, not acted on a stage? And it's written in a language that's hard to understand in English, let alone Hebrew. This production is going nowhere. This director is an idealistic dreamer who has religious fantasies.*

At least religious fantasies are better than romantic ones. Religious ones usually come true. If not, people always say "it was God's will," or "I'm being punished for my sins" or some other such nonsense. But it's no fantasy that Isaac just ignored me in a most insulting manner. I wanted conversation; I got rudeness. I want to act in a play. I get a part in a drama no one, except our unwilling relatives, will pay a penny to see. The audience will want action, and we'll give them boring biblical poetry. My sister is driving everyone nuts about Oklahoma, and I want a gorgeous guy to notice me; then I find out he can't even answer an obvious question. He thinks he's a good actor because he's been in some Shakespearean plays in England; I think this will be the summer of my discontent.

Danny O' Halloran

The "Gingie"

June 1956

I sit at the counter of the café and study the young faces of the actors who are taking their seats at the scattered tables. I can't believe their lack of knowledge about their own heritage, their lack of enthusiasm for their own history, and their lack of interest in classical literature. They think that anything that happened before 1948 has little relevance. Until yesterday they didn't even know who John Milton was, and Samson and Delilah were just ancient biblical characters who happened to live in their hometown, along with a multitude of others. None of these characters are as dynamic as the modern day heroes they admire. They love to talk about Moshe Dayan, Chaim Weitzman, or David Ben Gurion. But anyone who lived, loved, or schemed before the twentieth century is utterly irrelevant as far as they are concerned.

Who did I think was important when I was 18? Frank Sinatra, Tommy Dorsey, Betty Grable, and the Andrews Sisters were my idols. My greatest dream was to own a souped-up Studebaker Golden Hawk convertible. But during my freshman year in college I developed a love for reading, which turned into a passion for classical British literature. Much to my surprise, as a senior at Cornell University, I won a Rhodes scholarship that enabled me to study seventeenth century English literature at Oxford University. I am used to the intense and scholarly British companions I've associated with for the past three years while doing research for my doctoral dissertation on John Milton. These barely educated Israelis know more about Uzi machine guns and Kalashnikov assault rifles than they do about literature and art.

I grin as I remember that when I asked them what Shakespearean works they had studied a girl named Tamar asked, "Didn't he write *Kiss Me Kate*?" I loved how upset she became when I roared with laughter.

Just then I hear a roar of laughter explode from the table where Hannah is chattering away in rapid-fire Hebrew with her friends. Simon, who is sitting beside her, looks at me and says something which makes everyone grin. The only word I understand is "gingie," which I've heard over and over since I arrived in Israel.

Last night I went to a kosher restaurant with some English-speaking friends and was completely bewildered when I saw that the menu was written entirely in Hebrew. Unable to decipher the strange Hebrew letters (it should be against international law for a menu to be written in any language except English), I was about to order salami on rye and a Coca-Cola (I figured those words are the same in every language on Earth) when the waiter snarled, "Gingie, what do you want? Hurry up, I don't have all day."

Taken aback by the waiter's rudeness, I politely said in perfect Hebrew a sentence I've been practicing all week just for an occasion like this. "I'll have a ham and cheese sandwich with a glass of milk, please."

The look on the waiter's face was priceless.

But an arrogant waiter calling me "gingie" is one thing. My cast is another. If they don't respect me now, before rehearsals begin in earnest, the play will be a total disaster.

I manage to catch Hannah's attention and motion to her to join me. Surprised, but pleased at being singled out from the group, she comes over to the counter and sits down on the stool beside me.

"Hannah, could you translate a Hebrew word for me?"

"Sure."

"What is a "gingie?"

"You're a gingie, Danny. I was told I was one when I was little, but I don't think I really was."

"Yes, but what is a gingie?"

"A redhead."

"A redhead?"

"A redhead. I was told I had red hair when I was very little. Now, I'm what you Americans call a strawberry blonde. Of all the Hebrew words why did you want to know what that one meant?"

"People have been calling me that since I came here."

"Well, redheads are rare in this part of the world. Israelis get all excited when they see one. Do you want to know why my mother says that a few Jews, and I think this must also be true for some Irish, have red hair and green eyes?"

"Why?"

"You see, the red-haired, green-eyed Vikings came down in the 7th or 8th century to southern and central Europe and Britain and raped many women. Since I have green eyes and a little tinge of red hair, and you have really red hair and green eyes, we must both have Viking blood in our veins."

"Ya, I heard dose Vikings ver nasty fellas. The black-haired, blue-eyed Celts ran away to Ireland to escape the Norsemen, but I guess my ancestors were a bit too slow."

She laughs, "I guess mine were, too." Then she smiles coquettishly at me. "Danny, are you absolutely determined to put on this play about Samson and Delilah? It's not too late to change to something lighter and more modern."

"Hannah, just as you are fascinated by American music, cowboys and Indians and the Wild West, I am fascinated by biblical history. Do you have any idea what it means to me to be in the land where Jesus walked, King David ruled, Saint Peter fished, and the Virgin Mary lived? *Oklahoma*, which I know you wish we were putting on, is about love of land and the love between a boy and a girl, but a biblical story like Samson and Delilah is that and more, much more. This type of story conveys a sense not only about man's relationship with the person and land he loves, but also with the God he loves and the responsibilities he has to his people."

"Danny, it's hot. It's summer. War's in the air. We tense Israelis have had a long relationship with our God. We need to relax and let our long red hair down. The last thing we need to do is be reminded of how we fought the Philistines centuries ago. If you want to relive a biblical experience, I'll take you to Jerusalem one day and you can walk the Stations of the Cross. Would you like that?"

"Is that a bribe?"

"Darn. You saw through me!"

"I'll tell you what. How about we perform *Samson Agonistes* first? If the play is a success, we'll use the profits immediately to mount a production of *Oklahoma*."

"You mean it?"

"My word of honor. I don't have to be back in Oxford until the end of September."

"Danny, you're just a guy who cain't say no."

"Not to a fellow Viking."

We grin conspiratorially at each other. "Hey, everybody," she yells to the cast, "Guess what the gingie says we can do?"

Isaac

THE NECKLACE

JUNE 1956

Before Rebecca can sit down beside Hannah and Simon, I motion to her to join me. She hesitates; I know I made a major mistake in the auditorium. I should have talked to her. How else am I going to gain her confidence? How else will I find out the information Omar wants me to get from her? I ask if she wants a Coke. She reluctantly nods; I order one for each of us.

"Look," I say in my most contrite manner, "I know I was rude to you in the auditorium. You asked me a question that upset me tremendously, and I couldn't answer you.

"You asked if the cycle of war ever ends. My uncle was killed in the first months of the 1948 war. My family, especially my mother, never forgot how her brother died. I have never stopped wanting to avenge his death. I loved him as much as I love my father. All I think about is killing those responsible for his death. Can you understand that?"

"I can, but consider this. If we keep killing those who kill us, war never stops. Revenge breeds revenge. And vengeance won't bring your uncle back. It won't bring any of the dead back. War only makes more people die. Don't you realize every peace treaty contains the seeds for the next war?"

There is a long awkward silence between us which, thankfully, is broken when Hannah gleefully announces that Danny has agreed to put on *Oklahoma* after our production of *Samson Agonistes*.

"I see Hannah has our director wrapped around her little finger," I tell Rebecca with my most charming smile.

"I knew she'd sweet-talk him into doing exactly what she wants. She's such a conniver. I don't have half the nerve she does."

"The two of you don't even look alike. It's hard to believe you're sisters. She's so fair, and you're so dark. You're so quiet and calm, and she's a bundle of nervous energy. And her chutzpah! She makes all the other sabras look modest and polite."

Rebecca gives me a strange look, and then she bends down to pick up a paper napkin that has fallen to the floor. I quickly reach down to pick it up for her, and as I do, I see the obverse side of the golden Star of David necklace she is wearing dangle in midair in front of the suggestive curves of her breasts. No Muslim girl would dress like this in public. While I find it difficult to avoid looking at her cleavage, I gently catch hold of her necklace and examine it closely very aware of how near my hand is to her chest.

"How fascinating," I say, and am sincere for the first time this afternoon. "This Star has a gold cross welded onto its back. I had no idea ecumenical jewelry like this was sold in Israel."

"You can't buy this anywhere. It's unique and has a very special story."

"Oh, you have to tell me. This is an unusual necklace."

"Well, it looks as if my sister and Simon are having another one of their arguments. I can't figure out if they spend more time arguing or making up."

I laugh. Then I take another look at both sides of the necklace before I let it rest in its proper place between her breasts.

Rebecca takes a long sip of her soda, then she leans back in her chair, fixing her gaze on me. I can see that she is debating whether or not she should tell me the story about her necklace. I look at her as though she is the only person in the world I care about, and give her my most genuine smile. Then I reach across the table and take her hand. This approach always worked with the English girls who acted with me in the Shakespearean plays I was in at college, but Rebecca regards me severely.

She takes her hand back, shakes her index finger at me, and says firmly, "First, you must promise never to tell Hannah any of this, or I can't tell you the story of my necklace."

Mystified, I nod my head. "I promise."

"If you tell her, you will upset her very much. And I do not ever want her to be upset. I love her dearly."

"You have my solemn word."

"And you must never tell Simon either. He loves Hannah, thinks she is a sabra, and I don't want him to know the truth about her."

"Why? Would it make him think less of her?"

"I'm not sure, but I can't take that chance. Simon has his prejudices."

"Now I'm totally confused. What connection does your necklace have with Simon loving or not loving Hannah?"

"Imagine that it is the first week of September in 1939. My mother and father are sitting with the rest of their family around the table just before lunch on the Sabbath. They have come home from the synagogue and, as usual, the entire family has gathered to spend the afternoon together. They are very excited because my mother has just announced that she thinks she has felt her first labor pain."

"Was that you kicking her?"

"No, it was a labor contraction, not a baby's kick. Don't you know anything about how babies are born?

"No'm, Miz Scarlett. I don't know nuthin' 'bout birthin' babies. Do you?"

She giggles. "Touché. Anyhow, the family, especially my father is very happy when, suddenly, my uncle Moses, who is deaf, comes running into the room signing that the ground is trembling. No one can understand what he means, but he is so agitated and so insistent that something terrible is happening that my father runs up to the third floor and looks out of one of the attic windows. Far in the distance he sees German tanks advancing toward the village and refugees fleeing in the opposite direction toward the Russian border."

"Hadn't your family heard about the German invasion of Poland?"

"They would not have listened to the radio Friday or Saturday because they were too religious to use any electrical appliances. The Germans invaded so quickly that the whole country was caught unawares. Everyone grabbed what few belongings he or she could and joined the throngs fleeing the area. Since my mother was in labor, everyone decided to give her and my father the one horse and cart belonging to the family."

"Why didn't they take a car?" I asked.

"They knew they wouldn't be able to buy gas anywhere. The horse could always find grass. My parents grabbed the few possessions they could load on the cart, said a hasty goodbye to their apprehensive relatives, and made plans to rejoin them in a Russian town called Novosibirsk, where we had a distant cousin. Of course, my parents had no idea how far they would have to travel to reach the Russian border. If they did reach it, which was unlikely, they had no idea where in Russia Novosibirsk was. It's a good thing they didn't know or they may have given up before they even started."

"Novosibirsk is in Siberia, isn't it?"

Rebecca nods. "By nightfall, my mother was having very painful labor contractions. And, to make matters even more difficult, it started to rain. My father knew he had to find help for my mother, but he was afraid to go to a Christian hospital in any of the towns they passed. Anyway, everyone seemed to be running away from the advancing German army. As they traveled through the deserted countryside he noticed a farmhouse in the middle of a field with a barn a few hundred feet to its left. The house was dark and he thought it was vacant. The barn door was open and he left my mother in the wagon while he cautiously walked over to the building to inspect it. He was surprised to find a few cows inside munching hay and a few chickens roosting in the rafters. But he saw no humans anywhere and guessed that the farmer and his family must have joined the throngs of refugees and left the animals for the Germans. Besides, he thought, the cows would have only slowed the farmer down. And who needs a few noisy hens when one is escaping the enemy?

"My mother thought it was a blessing that the cows and chickens were in the barn. She thought they could milk the cows and gather a few eggs in the morning before they began their journey. All my father could think about was the baby."

"What happened next?"

"My father took some blankets from the cart and made a makeshift bed for my mother on the floor of the barn. Somehow he delivered me. He told me I was the ugliest yet most beautiful baby he had ever seen. Beautiful because I was alive and had all my fingers and toes. Ugly because I looked like him instead of my mother, and he couldn't wash the blood and mucus from me."

"I think you are quite beautiful even if you do look like your father."

"Thank you. I have my father's nose and eyes."

"Your dark eyes are lovely and your nose is exquisite."

"Whenever my father says I was an ugly newborn because I looked like him, I think he is fishing for a compliment."

"And you aren't?"

"Of course not."

We both laugh. "Then how did you and your parents get to Siberia?" I ask.

"I never did. Don't get ahead of the story."

"I'm sorry. Go on."

"After I was born my father wrapped me in his undershirt. It was the only soft cotton cloth he had. My parents had left their home in such a hurry that they forgot all the little necessities they should have taken. Then he and my mother fell into an exhausted sleep."

"I can well imagine."

"The next thing they knew a strange, red-haired, green-eyed man was standing over them. Startled, my father stood up and held me protectively in his arms."

"The missing farmer?"

"Exactly. It was obvious the man was not Jewish, especially since a large golden cross was hanging around his neck. As the Christians were known for their fervent anti-Semitism, my father was petrified. The man looked at my father, at my mother, and then at me. He stared at my mother's Star of David that she wore around her neck and then asked, "Do you want some breakfast?""

"He didn't turn them in to the Germans? Obviously not, because you are all here."

"No, he brought them some coffee, bread, and eggs from the farmhouse. After my surprised and appreciative parents thanked him profusely and gratefully ate the meal, he made an astounding proposal to them. He told them that the Germans were inspecting every house and rounding up all the Jews. My parents would have to hide in the woods, which would be impossible with a newborn baby."

"Your mother and father must have been desperate."

"Absolutely frantic. And then the farmer told them something they couldn't believe. He said that during the night his own wife had delivered a baby. It was her third child, and both of them were overjoyed because she had two previous miscarriages. She went to sleep thanking God for her beautiful little girl. The farmer told them that he had put the baby in a crib beside their bed and gazed at her for a long time until he, too, fell asleep.

But when he woke up early this morning he looked at his daughter and saw, to his great dismay and disbelief, that she was dead. He quickly took her tiny dead body out of the room so his wife wouldn't see it when she opened her eyes. He had come to the barn to find some wood to make a coffin and to get a shovel to dig a grave for the child. As grief-stricken as he was over the death of his child, he was more concerned about how his wife would react. He truly feared for her sanity. When he saw us he thought we were a gift from God."

"Why?"

"He told us that his wife was still asleep and didn't know the child was dead. He begged my parents to give me to him. He said he was afraid his wife would have a nervous breakdown if she discovered that her third child had died. 'You will never be able to hide from the Germans with a newborn infant. You will never reach a place of safety before your baby's cries will betray you,' he told my father. 'With me, she has a chance to live. So will you. And so will my wife.'"

"And your parents agreed to give you up?"

"My mother took off her Star of David necklace and gave it to the farmer. She made him promise that he would tell me that I was Jewish and that they loved me very much. Then she said they sympathized with him about his wife, but if they survived the war they would come back for me. If he didn't agree to give me up to them after the war, they would not give me to him now."

"He probably figured your parents would never make it."

"Of course. But he surprised them by taking off his gold cross and giving it to them. 'Wear my gold cross,' he told them. 'It will keep you safe from the Germans until the war is over. When you give me back my cross I will give you back your daughter and your Star of David.'"

"Unbelievable! He didn't have to do that."

"My Polish father, Yanek Slavinsky, was an incredible human being. He thought that in a few years he would tell his wife, Marta, what he had done, and she would be able to deal with the loss of her real daughter better then."

"Did she?"

"He never told her. Everyone wondered how people who were so fair could have a daughter who was so dark. He told the villagers that he had an aunt living in Cracow who was a dark-haired beauty, and that I looked just like her. The war dragged on; he never heard a word from my parents and he assumed that they were dead. Just as the war ended my Polish mother became pregnant again. This time Yanek took her to Cracow, and she gave birth in a hospital, attended by a doctor. She had a lovely little reddish-blonde baby girl with green eyes."

"Not Hannah? Incredible!"

Rebecca nodded. "But there was a tuberculosis epidemic in Cracow, and the hospital was full of patients with the disease. I imagine the quarantine conditions were not strictly observed because my mother came down with a terminal case. Back then everyone who became ill with tuberculosis died because the antibiotics to cure it weren't available in Poland. So Hannah lived, but my Polish mother died."

"Yanek must have been devastated. He had done what he thought was best for his wife, and it killed her."

"And he nursed her so devotedly that he caught the disease from her. When he became very ill, he didn't know what to do. All his relatives had died in the war. He didn't want to place us in an orphanage, and he was sure that children were starving and mistreated in the refugee camps. Besides, we weren't really refugees."

"Were children mistreated in the refugee camps?"

"I have no idea. He was just sure no one could love us or take care of us as well as he did. But I had started to nurse him, and he was afraid that I would catch the disease from him, so he made arrangements for us to go to a convent. I would attend its school, and the nuns would care for Hannah in their nursery. A few days before we were to leave for the convent two strange men came to the farm. I gazed at the older man and thought I was seeing, for the first time, someone who looked like me and felt like me."

"Your father?"

"My father. He and my mother had made it to the border and my father joined the Russian Partisans and fought against Germany throughout the war. My mother and the rest of the family lived in a small village in the southwestern part of Siberia in the Altai Mountains. They couldn't come for me right after the war because Stalin wouldn't allow the Jews to leave. Then, in 1946, there was a window of a few weeks in which any Polish Jew who had fought with the Partisans in the Russian army could return to Poland. Since my father had fought in the Russian underground we qualified.

"My parents, together with my brother, David, who was born three years after my parents fled to Siberia, left Russia immediately and went to Stettin, Poland. They knew there was no point in going back to their village since the devastation from the war was horrendous. Conditions in Stettin were so bad for the Jews they decided to immigrate to Israel. As soon as he could, my father and his younger brother came looking for me."

"The farmer must have been overjoyed to see them."

"He was ecstatic. But he told them that if his wife had not died, and if he were not so ill, he did not think they could ever have given me back, for they loved me dearly, and I adored them. How could I not? I believed they were my real parents. He had never told me who I really was because he was sure my parents could not have survived the war."

"How did you feel when you found out the truth?"

"Terribly confused. First of all, I was still upset that my Polish mother had died. I was frantic when my Polish father told me he was dying and that Hannah, who was only ten months old, and I were going to a convent. I didn't even know what a convent was, and I was terribly frightened of the nuns, who wore black robes and veils that completely covered their hair. Can you imagine how I felt when he told me that he was not my real father and that this dark stranger was? Then he did something that I will never forget. He took this golden Star of David from a box he had secreted away on a high shelf in his bedroom closet and gave it to my father."

"This necklace?"

"Yes. My father took the gold cross the Polish farmer had given him so many years ago, kissed it, and then put it around the dying man's neck. He told my Polish father that the cross had saved his life several times."

"But how did the cross come to be soldered onto the Star of David?"

"My Polish father took the cross off his neck and gave it back to my real father. He said, and this is engraved forever in my memory, 'Now, I have a favor to ask you. Save my Hannah as I saved your daughter. Raise her as lovingly as I raised yours. But since I can never reclaim her, raise her as a Jewess. I do not want her to have the feeling that she is a stranger in a strange land, as Rebecca would have if I had told her who her real parents were.' I will never forget his face and how he looked at me when he said those words."

Her voice broke, and a tear slowly rolled down her cheek. She grasped the necklace in her hand and turned it over so she could see the cross. "My Polish father did not want Hannah to have this. He felt the Israelis would ostracize her if they knew she wasn't Jewish. We hide her identity from her to protect her."

"He was a very wise man."

"Yes, but he still wanted my father to have it as a symbol of what the two men had done for each other. My father told the farmer that a few times Germans had stopped him, and when they saw the gold cross around his neck they let him go on his way. Now he would be rescuing Hannah from an orphanage. So my father took it and told the farmer that he would attach it to the back of my mother's Star of David and give it to me as a symbol of the Christian family who had loved me and the Jewish family who will love his daughter."

"But something is still missing from your necklace."

"What?"

"Palestine is the land of three faiths. You should also have a Muslim crescent attached to your necklace."

"Isaac, I'm a little too old for another mother and father."

"Who said anything about a foster parent? How about a Muslim husband?"

"Isaac! How could you say such a thing? What would **your** father say if you came home with a Muslim wife?"

I look at her seriously. "I think he would be more upset if I came home with a Christian wife."

"Oh, Isaac, don't think because I wear this necklace that has a cross on it that I would marry a Christian."

"Good. That eliminates a lot of competition. You won't marry a Christian or a Muslim. Now I only have to watch out for all the handsome Jewish men in Ashkelon."

"Well, you can definitely eliminate the most handsome man I know."

"And who is that?"

"Simon. He only has eyes for Hannah. That's why you must never tell either of them this story."

"Why? Don't you think he will still love her even if he knows she was born to Christian parents? After all, she was raised as a Jew since she was an infant. At the very least, shouldn't Hannah know the truth about herself?"

"Her own father didn't want her to consider herself an outsider, or know that she is an adopted child. He knew how estranged that might make her feel, and he wanted to spare her those emotions. A Protestant couple had adopted the son of his dark-haired Catholic aunt who hoped to save the child from the Nazis who were arresting people on any pretext. He didn't want his daughter to experience the same psychological problems that little boy did.

"Simon is an avid Zionist whose family suffered more persecution from the Poles than from the Germans. Polish villagers found two of his uncles, who had been hiding in a forest for four years, and turned them over to the Germans a few hours before the war was over rather than let them be rescued by Russian soldiers who were about to eliminate German presence from that area.

"A few weeks later he went into a Polish store to buy some soap. He told us that the clerk and the Polish people in the store laughed at him when the salesperson handed him the bag which contained a few bars of soap. When Simon came home and handed the soap to his mother she started to cry and told him the letters on the soap indicated they were made from the fat of Jewish prisoners who had been killed in the concentration camp at Auschwitz. He watched his parents bury the bars of soap and say *Kaddish*[1] over them."

"How horrible! How old was he?"

"About six. He never forgot that incident and he never forgot how cruel the Poles had been toward his family. They had been very rich and the Poles drove them from their house, their orchards, their herds, everything they had. We feel that if he knew that Hannah was the child of Christian Poles, he would subconsciously hold it against her. We don't lie; we just don't tell him the truth."

I give her my most charming, charismatic smile. "Now, that I know Simon is not competing with me for your hand, do I have a chance?"

Rebecca laughs, "We've known each other for a few days. Do you think we could give ourselves at least a week?"

"Playing hard to get?" I smile.

"Absolutely!"

"Oh, where are the women like Juliet? Juliet, Juliet, wherefore art thou? She loved Romeo at first sight."

"Yes, and look what happened to them."

"Ah, they may have been star-crossed, but they truly loved each other," I protest.

"You are a romantic."

"And you are a practical realist."

"I intend to live long," Rebecca states firmly. "Romantic love is very nice, but its flame burns brightly for a short while and then reality sets in."

"And that is...?"

"Dirty diapers, crying babies, war, sickness, debts, gray hair or even worse, baldness."

"Enough. Maybe we should die young, before I grow bald and you get gray hair."

---

1 A prayer a Jew says to commemorate the memory of a dead relative. Members of the Jewish community will recite this prayer for any dead person who has no living relative who can perform the ritual. It is said every day for a year after a person dies and then every year on the anniversary of his or her death.

"You may grow bald, but who said the gray hair would be mine? I will never get fat, gray, or old," Rebecca says in mock indignation.

"No, age will never wither you, nor custom stale your infinite variety." I look so steadily into her eyes that she blushes and looks away.

"Isn't that a quote from Shakespeare?"

"It's from *Antony and Cleopatra*. Like Delilah, Cleo was a fascinating temptress and Antony adored her.

"You think I'm a fascinating temptress? Is that a compliment or an insult?"

At that moment we hear Danny call, "Okay, group, let's go back to rehearsal."

This time I will recite my part to Danny's satisfaction. If I charm Rebecca, she will tell me more, much more than intriguing tales of her childhood. I watch her walk over to Hannah and Simon, who are still arguing. Hannah finally shrugs her shoulders, leaves Simon, and walks out of the restaurant with Rebecca.

I wait a few seconds, before diplomatically falling into step with Simon. I realize that he is someone I should cultivate as a friend, since he is not only close to the Silverman family, but also a paratrooper. As we begin to walk together I ask cautiously, "Trouble with Hannah?"

Simon answers, "She is upset because I just told her my furlough is over after our final performance of *Samson Agonistes*. She wants me to ask for an extension so we can act together in *Oklahoma*."

"Isn't that impossible?"

"To Hannah, nothing is impossible. She says if we petition her uncle and say we're going to do the play as entertainment for the troops, I'd be allowed to act in it and extend my leave."

"Can you do that?"

"She knows the only reason David and I are on leave now is our unit is scheduled for special combat training when it's up."

"Do you think there will be war soon?"

"At this minute I'd rather have war with Egypt than with Hannah."

I laugh. When I pass Omar, who is still sitting at the café's sidewalk table, I give him a barely perceptible nod as I slowly walk across the street and into the building where, surrounded by Israelis, I ascend the stairs to center stage.

Rebecca

REVERIES

JUNE 1956

How could I have told Isaac the story about Hannah? I don't even know him. Ten minutes ago I thought he was a handsome, empty shell who couldn't carry on an intelligent conversation. First, he ignored me, then he charmed me. When he looked into my eyes with utmost sincerity, held my hand with great tenderness, and looked at my Star of David with profound interest, I couldn't resist telling him our greatest family secret. Does he really care for me? He is charismatic, but until now, he gave me the feeling that he thought I'm beneath him. As rehearsal began, I thought that he couldn't stand to be in the same room with the rest of us, especially Danny.

Did I tell him the secret about Hannah and me because I am attracted to him? Why do I even care what he thinks about me? Why did I want to explain to him why I wear a Christian cross? He's better-looking than Simon, but I'll never let him know that. There's something sinister and intriguing about him, yet, at the same time, something appealing and sensitive. When he sat down next to me, looked at me with his dark, bottomless eyes, and bought me a Coke, I felt drawn to him as I have never felt drawn to anyone else.

At the audition he read his speech as if he were born to act; today he said his lines so badly I wondered what was wrong with him. I almost felt, as we rehearsed, that he hated me, or that he hated being in the hall with us. Yet, here in the café, he was friendly and considerate. He even joked about marrying me. Custom does not stale his infinite variety, either. He obsesses me; he fascinates me; he captivates me.

This may be a wonderful summer, or not. Who knows? But if we do put on *Oklahoma*, I want to be Laurie to his Curly. Hannah will be the girl who just cain't say no, but in odd, intriguing way, Isaac compels me to say yes, yes, yes!

Ishmael

THE CHARADE CONTINUES

JUNE 1956

It's the Israeli Sabbath. The one-room apartment the Egyptian military intelligence office obtained for me is suffocating and claustrophobic. It's sparsely furnished, with a simple bed in one corner. A spindly table and two chairs are in the center of the room, and a hot plate on a counter under the one window serves as a poor excuse for a kitchen. A fan can barely blow a little cool air toward my bed. I try to get more relief from the oppressive heat by opening the refrigerator door and aiming the fan's blades toward the cooling coils of the ancient appliance. I soak my undershirt in cold water, slip it on, and stand between the refrigerator and the fan. The cooling sensation is welcome but brief, for my shirt dries in the arid heat as fast as Omar loses his temper.

I chuckle as I thought how glamorous and intriguing the life of a spy would be after I read *Casino Royale*, the novel Ian Fleming, one of my fellow students at Sandhurst, wrote. All our classmates at the British military academy avidly devoured the pages which describe how James Bond wears tuxedos, drinks martinis which are shaken, not stirred, plays baccarat in Monte Carlo and makes love to beautiful but dangerous women. Bond knows immediately what he should do in any situation, and he always destroys his enemies. Enviably, 007 has the use of the latest technological devices and drives the most fantastic cars. He would never be assigned to an apartment like this, nor would he be trying to cool himself by sitting in front of an antique refrigerator as an asthmatic fan blows on his dripping wet undershirt.

I wipe the sweat off my forehead and think, *Where did I go wrong? I am one of those poor deluded readers who thought the life of a spy is dangerous and glamorous. All the cadets at Sandhurst who are interested in military intelligence imagine that they can be as suave and urbane as Ian Fleming's Bond. In reality, spying is demoralizing, boring, perilous, and damned uncomfortable.*

At least, that girl Rebecca is pretty. In fact, she could seduce James Bond easily. But Bond wears a tuxedo as he gambles on the Riviera, while I have to pretend I want to be in a xenophobic play with arrogant Israelis who can't act.

Sighing, I pick up the script of *Samson and Delilah* and begin to study it. I remember yesterday's rehearsal with irritation and silently curse Omar for forcing me to be in this ridiculous play in a flea-bitten, sand trap of a town.

The director, Danny O'Halloran, was very unhappy with my reading of some of the lines. I was really annoyed when he sat me down in front of the entire cast and tried to make me understand Samson's character. At first, I did my best to pretend to be interested in the director's attempt to motivate me to emote more expressively.

But then, he had no idea how much his talk affected me. When he said, "Can you imagine how Samson must have felt? Even before his birth, his fate had already been determined. Don't you remember that an angel appeared to his mother and told her that her unborn son was going to be the champion of the Hebrews and deliver them from the oppression of their Philistine neighbors?

"How you would feel if you could make no decisions for yourself? Your destiny has been decided for you, your way of life is rigidly prescribed, and you have no free will. If you deviate in any way, the spirit of the Lord will forsake you. Are you defiant, resentful, resigned, or accepting?"

The irony of the situation is almost ludicrous. I realized that the only difference between Samson and me was that the ancient

Biblical judge's parents did not arrange his marriage for him. At least Samson picked his own wives. Perhaps if they had demanded that he marry a Hebrew woman his life would have been less calamitous. But the impulsive and rash Samson chose love over a prudent, sensible, and discreet existence. Stupid guy.

Aloud, I said to Danny, "I guess Samson was rebellious."

"He probably was. Instead of marrying a woman from his own tribe, he married a Philistine woman, and as the Bible tells us he consorted with a harlot in Gaza before his relationship with Delilah. I doubt, even though the Bible doesn't say so, that he limited himself to just one harlot. Since the Jews are known to be stringently against intermarriage, these relationships may have been the one form of defiance that was open to him.

"Nevertheless," Danny continued, "He did kill many Philistines, but only when he felt they personally humiliated him, not because he was trying to protect his people. He was a vengeful and arrogant man whose brute strength was far greater than his ethical integrity.

"You have to depict a tragic man who, at his death, humiliated, blinded, enslaved, and tortured by his enemies, was able to realize his faults and redeem himself and finally fulfill his destiny. Now, see if you can convey all this to the audience. It's a tall order, I know, to ask of an amateur actor but, for God's sake, try."

And then he gave me a pat on the back.

I hate to be lectured in front of people, and that pat was more patronizing than encouraging. Mercifully, he ended the rehearsal shortly thereafter. I told him I would read the lines with more feeling on Monday. I don't know whom I should hate more: Omar for forcing this assignment on me, or John Milton for writing this play which depicts how Samson loved unwisely and too well, and then killed his wife and everyone else who crossed him.

Oklahoma is really beginning to appeal to me.

Restless, resentful, and unable to concentrate, I throw the script on the bed and begin pacing around the sizzling hot room that the fan, which was old when Samson was flexing his biceps for Delilah, is unable to cool. Finally, I throw on a white sport shirt over my now dry undershirt and go out into the baking street, which shimmers in the heat. I head for the park beside the café where I first saw Rebecca and her family. I know that many Israelis promenade on the main street after their Sabbath lunch. I hope I will meet the Silverman family, partly because I want to finish this assignment as quickly as possible and leave Ashkelon, and partly because I want to see Rebecca again. Never before have I met a girl who possesses her aura of quiet beauty allied with an inner reserve of steel. This resolute strength, combined with her graceful serenity, interests me. Behind her tranquil nature she has a sense of melancholy that serves as a reminder of the troubled times which afflict both our cultures. Yet, she is so innocent and trusting that I know it will be easy to obtain information about her brother's and uncle's military movements. Hannah's comic nature and what the Israelis call chutzpah amuse me. But Rebecca's loveliness and youthful naiveté, combined with her pensive, sad nature, is both attractive and captivating. Besides, I'm lonely.

But, it's dangerous to be in such close quarters with Israelis. I remember that I had almost blown my cover a few weeks ago when I was on assignment in the town of B'nai Berak, where extremely religious Jews live. The people there are so devout that even the atheists pray on the Sabbath! I saw an emaciated skeleton of an old man, who, despite the oppressive heat, was dressed in the traditional white, long-sleeved shirt, black pants, black jacket, and ridiculous-looking fur-trimmed hat of his orthodox sect coming toward me. His long, black, coiled forelocks bobbed up and down with every step he took, and his curly beard blanketed his perspiring cheeks. I have no idea why he was wearing his threadbare black coat on such a hot day unless it was to prevent me from counting his ribs, which protruded through its cheap fabric.

I'm quite used to seeing these strange Jews dressed in the garb of the eighteenth-century founder of their movement, but this one was unusual for he was limping with great difficulty beside a lively, sturdy-looking donkey down the middle of the street. As I approached him, the man called out, "Shabbat Shalom[2]."

"Shabbat Shalom," I replied, "Why are you walking beside the donkey? You look exhausted. Why don't you ride on him?

The man glared at me indignantly. "I'm taking him for his Sabbath walk. You know it's forbidden to ride animals today. Didn't you learn that the Bible commands us to give not only our servants, but also our animals their Sabbath rest? Where do you come from?"

The donkey glared at me as if to say "What an ass!" and the two of them slowly promenaded down the street in tandem.

A more blatant mistake made towards a more cautious and sharp-witted Israeli could arouse suspicions I didn't need aroused.

Vowing that I will not make any mistakes which could make the residents of Ashkelon wary about me, I head to the main thoroughfare, where I notice that more men and women than usual are in military uniform, even though it's the Sabbath. Suddenly, despite the glare of the blinding noonday sun, I see Rebecca walking to the café, which surprisingly, is open on the Sabbath, accompanied by her entire family. Even her older brother and uncle are in uniform. They sit at an outdoor table where I can easily watch them. Again, I am faced with the same conundrum:

How do I make people I hate like me?

How can I pretend to like people I hate?

I know I will have to think of a way to go over to them and initiate a conversation when Rebecca solves my problem by coming over to me.

"Shabbat Shalom," she says, smiling shyly.

"Shabbat Shalom," I answer, smiling back at her.

"There is a law that no one is allowed to spend Saturday afternoon alone in Ashkelon. So, I've come to enforce the law by asking you to join us for a cool drink."

"I can't break the law. Not when the enforcer is so pretty."

---

2 Shabbat Shalom is a traditional greeting reserved for the Sabbath. It means: May you have a day of rest filled with peace.

"I must warn you. My sister, Hannah, is the police chief."

I hold up my hands in mock surrender and smilingly follow her to the table.

"Isaac, these are my parents, my brothers, David and Jonathan, and my Aunt Rachel and Uncle Yossi Ben Dassan." As the men rise from their seats and shake hands with me, I realize I am so nervous about actually sitting down with Israelis that I am perspiring profusely. For once, I am glad it is hot. I nod awkwardly at the two women and Hannah. I don't know if I am supposed to shake their hands as well.

Inwardly I panic, *Here's another situation no one briefed me on. Israeli women are so independent; they may be used to shaking hands with men and think I am rude if I don't offer to do so with them.*

But the women stay seated and give me a pleasant, but brief acknowledgement as they continue to talk animatedly with one other.

The three men, the young boy, and Rebecca sit down, and I take the empty seat beside her and try to look as calm and self-assured as James Bond would be if he were here.

"So, what would you like to drink? Something ice-cold?" her father asks me as he beckons to a waitress to take their order.

"A chocolate ice cream soda."

"Me, too," said Hannah.

David and Rebecca laugh uproariously.

"Did I say something wrong?" I ask.

"No, no, no. Before you came we were just teasing Hannah that she will get fat from drinking too many ice cream sodas," Rebecca says with a meaningful pinch at her sister's slightly chubby cheek.

"I will not get fat. I dance two hours a day."

"Two hours a day! In this scorching weather!" I exclaim. "It's too hot to do that, even indoors."

As I continue to make small talk with the family, I notice that Omar takes a seat at a table about ten feet to my right and gives a brief order to the waitress. He studiously ignores looking at our table, but I know he is keenly observing us.

The general turns to his brother-in-law and complains, "My wife agrees with this young man. Your sister wants me to commute from Ashkelon to Hazor because she says it's too hot at home."

"Isn't your home here in Ashkelon?" I ask.

"No," replies the general. "We live in Hazor at the air force base."

"Do you stay there all year long?"

"Of course, except when my wife manages to drag me to Ashkelon to visit our relatives who live near the beach."

"And," Rachel interjected, "tomorrow I'm dragging him to visit our cousins who live in Caesaria. That's where I want to live when Yossi retires."

"Naturally, my wife picks the most expensive place in Israel for us to retire."

"No, I pick the most beautiful place."

The general sighs, "She'd rather put up with our relatives who live near beautiful beaches than stay in Hazor. She calls it the Oven of Israel, but it's the best training base in the entire country."

"I heard that," snaps Rebecca's father, Aaron. "You think I don't know why you visit us. You don't want to see me. You want to go to the beach. After all, what's so great about spending time with your sister and brother-in-law? You never call; you never write; then your wife decides she'd like a vacation at the beach, and, suddenly, you remember that you have relatives." Aaron pouts like an angry little child, but I can see that he is fond of his sister and brother-in-law and is only teasing them.

"Do they always argue like this?" I whisper to Rebecca.

"No," she whispers back. "They're just warming up. They get better as the day gets hotter."

"Where are you from, Isaac?" Rebecca's Aunt Rachel asks me.

"I was born in Jerusalem, but I've been living in England since I was a very young child. My father was offered a professorship in mathematics at Sandhurst when I was 11. I went to school there and just graduated from the military academy. I hope my family will return and live in Jerusalem again when his tenure is over."

"Why doesn't he apply to teach at Hebrew University in Jerusalem, or the Technion in Haifa?" asks the general.

"My mother would love that. She dreams of returning to Jerusalem."

At that moment the waitress brings the drinks and pastries. After a long cool sip of my soda I wipe my perspiring brow and turn to David, "I see you're a paratrooper. Where did you do your training?"

"Near Beersheva – the Oven of the Negev!"

Everyone laughs but David.

"Really, Beersheva's not the oven of Israel, Eilat is. I've been stationed there for the last two years, and it is so hot a person can burn his hands if he picks up a metal tool that's been lying in the sun for more than a few minutes. Once I had to change a tire on a jeep. I put the tire iron down on the sand and got a third-degree burn when I picked it up ten minutes later.

"Yet the desert has a magnificent beauty that no other part of Israel can match," he continues. "The sunsets are incredible; the Red Sea, you know, is really red because the water reflects the glow from the red rocks that line the shore. At night the air is so cool, and the stars are so bright and...."

"And there's sand, sand, everywhere and not a drop to drink," laughs Hannah. "I agree with you, Aunt Rachel. Anything south of Ashkelon is an oven and Eilat is the hottest one of all."

"Did I ever tell you, Hannah, that puns are the lowest form of humor?" asks David.

"That's not a pun, dummy. That's a parody. Don't you know the difference?"

"Uncle Yossi, if I strangled Hannah, do you think any jury in the world would convict me?" David asks in a mock-serious tone.

"They probably would want to know what took you so long."

Everyone laughs and I relax enough to join in.

David turns to me and asks the one question I have been dreading to hear, "What are you doing here in Ashkelon now? Do you want to go to the beach, too?"

I have prepared an answer which I hope they will believe. "After graduation from Sandhurst, I returned to Israel to do my army service. The second day I was here I met some of my old friends from Jerusalem and we had a wild soccer game. I scored a goal and was thrilled for about three seconds until I realized that my great kick had ruptured the Achilles tendon in my right foot. I injured it so badly I had to have immediate surgery and wore a cast for five weeks. When the surgeon took the cast off I had to wear a shoe boot another six weeks. Now, I'm going to physical therapy and as soon as the doctor clears me I'm going to Tel Nof Academy near Rehovot for basic training.

"In the meantime I'm so damn bored and restless I became interested in archaeology. The real reason I came to Ashkelon and tried out for the play is that this was the home of Samson. I started to do research about him and the Roman and Philistine artifacts in Ashkelon, especially the ancient wall and the tower at the outskirts of the town by the sea. If I'm lucky I might be able to sell the article to *National Geographic*. I've read so many of those issues in the doctor's office that I'd like to try to write an article and submit it to the magazine."

"What's so interesting about that wall?" asks Hannah.

"The tribe of Judah built it after a battle during which the Hebrews captured Ashkelon from the Philistines. This was when the Jews were ruled by judges and were a loose confederation of tribes, a long time before the reign of King David."

"Is it as old as that?" asks Rebecca. "I thought it only dated from the time of the Romans."

General Ben Dassan answers, "Not at all. The wall was old already before Abraham, Isaac, and Jacob lived here. It contains a two-story arched city gate which is the oldest one is the world. Didn't you know that King Herod was born in Ashkelon and built public baths, splendid palaces, and a first rate aqueduct somewhere near the beach?"

See," he says with a wink at his brother in law, "I'm not the only one who came here to the beach to escape the heat."

"Tomorrow," I announce, "after rehearsal, I'd like to go to the ruins. But I don't know my way around Ashkelon very well, and I don't have a car."

The general stares at me intently. "What else do you do besides write articles about ruins and play soccer?"

"All my life I've loved flying. I've flown small planes but I want to be a jet fighter pilot in the Israeli Air Force. Even though I was accepted at the British Royal Air Force Academy at Cranwell, my father, since he teaches at Sandhurst, insisted I go there. Now that I'm in Israel, maybe I can apply to the jet pilot training program after I finish basic training."

Rebecca whispers to me as her male relatives nod approvingly, "You just scored your first hit."

Hannah, who I can see enjoys embarrassing her sister whenever she has the opportunity, says teasingly (and falls into my trap), "Rebecca, why don't you take Isaac to see the ruins tomorrow after rehearsal?"

Much to her younger sister's surprise and my relief, Rebecca does not blush or stammer, but turns earnestly to me and says, "We can't go after rehearsal; it's too hot. Can you go early in the morning? It's really too hot after 11 to do anything but go to the beach. I can see why King Herod built baths and aqueducts here. Besides, don't you remember that Danny cancelled rehearsal for Sunday morning because he wants to go to a Christian church service in Jerusalem?"

Aunt Rachel asks Sarah in a low voice which I know is deliberately loud enough for me to hear, "Do you think she'll be safe wandering around those ruins with a stranger?"

I smile charmingly at her. "Don't worry, Mrs. Ben Dassan. I, Isaac Ben Abraham, personally guarantee her safety."

Hannah adds, "And just to be on the safe side, I think I should go along as a chaperone."

"No." Rebecca shakes her finger at her sister. "You won't be a chaperone. You'll be a pest. I think that you, David, and Jonathan should join us later at the beach. You two can pack a picnic lunch for us while I show Isaac those ancient ruins."

Hannah beams. I gather that she is not often included in her older brother and sister's plans. "How about I ask the dance group to join us at the picnic and we can do a little dancing later in the afternoon when it's cooler? Simon can lug his accordion and Jonathan will probably have his guitar. If Ben brings his clarinet, and Ruben takes one of his small drums, we can have our whole troupe dance some routines. And David doesn't have to report back to Eilat until Wednesday. I can even tell Danny O'Halloran to join us at the beach in the afternoon when he comes back from Jerusalem. He can decide which dance we can do in the temple scene."

Rebecca sighs, "Don't forget to invite the whole town to watch you. Gee, Hannah, you never do things in a small way, do you? I just wanted a small lunch after we look at the ruins. And now you're planning to invite half the people we know. Why can't I have an asocial, apathetic sister instead of a gung-ho social butterfly?"

But she smiles so sweetly as she teases her sister that Hannah knows she can invite her dance troupe and anyone else she wants to the beach, and Rebecca will welcome all of them, even her little brother Jonathan.

I look at the two sisters who are lovingly joking with each other, and I suddenly compare their relationship to mine with my sisters and brother. I realize how deeply each one cares about the other. Rebecca's story about Hannah's birth moved me more than I care to admit. I sense that Hannah is not worried about Rebecca's reputation as a proper Egyptian girl should be, but she wants to come to the beach because she truly enjoys her sister's company. I can see that David really doesn't want to go to the beach, but he will do anything his sisters want, not because he is worried about the family's honor, but because he likes to be with them and their friends.

Suddenly, I am filled with envy. I know my parents love my siblings and me. But our relationship is formal. I can't remember my mother ever joking with us. My father is always preoccupied with military affairs; my mother and sisters have never involved him in their plans, and my father, brother, and I have always regarded their conversation and daily activities as feminine frivolity beneath our dignity. We go to the club, play tennis with our friends, have tea, and socialize within our narrowly prescribed circle.

My fiancée is one of my sister's friends and the daughter of one of my father's colleagues. Our parents arranged the marriage during a dinner without even asking either of us how we felt about each other. They knew we had to concur with their decision. After all, their marriages had been arranged, and as far as I know, the marriages of my ancestors for generations had been loveless, political, and financial couplings which benefited the family name and fortunes, but not the heart. All the respectable men in our family were expected to have affairs, and all the dowry-rich women were expected to have sons who would carry on the family name, the family fortune, and their fathers' philandering ways.

In fact, I know my fiancée's father better than I know her. I can sense immediately that Rebecca, Hannah, and David would never allow their parents to select spouses for them. And even though Aunt Rachel expresses concern that I am going alone with Rebecca to the ruins and Hannah jokes about accompanying us, I know that the family would never send a chaperone with Rebecca, and that if they did, she would be embarrassed and indignant. And I also know that if I went alone with my fiancée she would be the one who would be extremely embarrassed and indignant that her family cared so little about her reputation that they would allow her to go unaccompanied into a public place.

All my life I believed that only my society treats women with respect, and that Muslim women who wear head scarves are modest, decent, and proper religious ladies. I am filled with distaste for the free-wheeling, jeans-wearing, tee-shirt attired, bare-headed, rifle-toting Israeli women, but I do admire their spirit of independence and their confidence. Do I want my fiancée to be like them? No! These are women who are equals, not subservient wives. While I like Rebecca's attitude, I do not want my wife to treat me the way Rachel and Sarah treat their husbands. Reason and intellect are fine qualities in a woman, but independence and spirit will cause disharmony in a home where the husband must be the master at all times. Gentleness, submissiveness, modesty, and spirituality are the qualities I want in a wife.

Still, I look forward to exploring the ancient ruins with Rebecca in the morning, and watching the two sisters dance on the beach after lunch. But I must get to know David better, and gain his and his uncle's confidence without raising any suspicions. And Omar's impatience is growing. I can sense it radiating from every perspiring pore in his body. It flows across the café's plaza into my vengeful being. Tomorrow cannot come quickly enough.

General Yassi Ben Dassan

A Wife's Suspicions

Later That Night

I have a brilliant wife who loves to have long, serious, conversations. Discussions about the most controversial topics such as politics, Jewish philosophy and religion, and the ever deteriorating Israeli-Arab situation obsess her. She resigns herself to having these discussions with her colleagues at the university where she teaches Hebrew literature because I dare not reveal to her the reasons behind the military and government policies that she so avidly questions.

We don't discuss religion since we hold differing religious points of view. I'm a born-again atheist and she believes in a God who I think has long abandoned his faithful.

Our only son died tragically at the age of five from viral equine encephalitis, a disease transmitted by a mosquito bite which did much to hasten my conversion to atheism; I can't believe in a God who demands the death of sons.

And as far as I am concerned, there will be a man on the moon long before there will be peace between the Arabs and the Jews, so arguing about the Middle East situation is a waste of time.

Arabs hate us. We hate them. Israelis feel this hate is fomented by Arab leaders in order to distract their peoples from the many social and economic problems which Lebanon, Syria, Egypt, Iraq, Iran and Jordan are unable or unwilling to solve. Arabs feel this is their land since it was part of the Ottoman Empire for hundreds of years.

Two people both want the same land. They greet each other with a word that means "peace" and all they feel for each other is loathing.

Therefore, to promote domestic tranquility between my wife and myself, we gossip about the latest African-American basketball athletes with the improbable Hebrew names of Patrick McGee and Shawn O'Hara who play for our Israeli teams. Finances and our relatives' activities are always safe topics. Although my brilliant wife considers these topics petty and trivial, she has resigned herself to our quiet, unexciting marital conversations. She knows I am a loving and faithful husband whose only interest is in military and political affairs which I cannot reveal to her.

Consequently, both of us have buried our grief over the death of our son and the knowledge that there are few topics of discussion in which we can converse freely by enveloping our lives fully in the affairs of our nieces.

"You know, Rachel," I remark to my wife as I leave my study and walk into the living room where she is reading a book, "That boy Rebecca introduced to us today is highly intelligent. He's just the kind of person who would make an excellent jet pilot. I am really impressed that he wants to write an article for a prestigious magazine about the ancient ruins of Ashkelon. But right now we don't need scholars; we need soldiers and pilots. I would love to have him come to Hazor after he learns to fly jets."

"Yossi, didn't you train in England at that school where the boy was accepted, Cranwell?"

"Of course. That's why I'm so impressed with him."

"Yossi, do you think you will be using those fighter jets very soon?"

I slam my fist emphatically on the coffee table in front of my wife as I list Israel's needs. "Rachel, if we don't lift the Egyptian blockade of the Straits of Tiran we can't trade with half the world. Think about it. India, China, Japan, and half of Africa can't reach our country and we can't sail to them. Also, we must stop the terrorist attacks of the Egyptian fedayeen. Our intelligence tells us that these terrorists are planning to make a major attack near here shortly. An air force with well-trained jet pilots is essential to combating the Egyptians. This Isaac Ben Abraham strikes me as a young man who will make an excellent pilot. He'll go far in the military. He could be a general someday. Men like him represent the future of our nation."

"And," Rachel smiles slyly at me, "you also think he'll make an excellent match for Rebecca."

"I can scheme against the entire international community and devise ingenious air force projects, but I can't fool you."

"Of course not. A woman's intuition is far superior to military intelligence. But, all joking aside, something about this Isaac bothers me."

"What?"

"I don't know exactly. He seems older than our David and Rebecca. He should have graduated from school years ago and be in the service already. And I can't place his accent. And did you notice how nervous he was?"

"Of course, he was nervous. You, Sarah, and Hannah were eyeing him as if he were ready to seduce Rebecca at any second. When you asked if it was safe to let him go to the ruins with her alone, I thought Rebecca was ready to strangle you.

"And why would he talk like a sabra? Remember he said he went to school in England. Don't forget we aren't sabras either, and we certainly don't have Israeli accents. You just met him for the first time, and already you want to know his entire history. You're hypercritical about anyone who may be interested in Rebecca."

"Yossi, there's something about him… Did you notice his eyes?"

"What about them?"

"They were never still. They were always either staring intently at one of us or looking uneasily around the square. And his last name bothers me. You know "Ben Abraham" is the name all converts take."

"Why do you assume he's a convert?

"He doesn't act Jewish. He acts like a, like a…"

I can see my sweet, tolerant wife searching her memory for all the bitter ethnic stereotypes she has stored up over the years as we fled from one European country to another until we came to Israel.

"Like a what?

"He acts like a Polack," she declares decisively.

"And what's wrong with Polish people?"

"You can't trust them. Look what they did to Simon's uncles."

"Yes, and Yanek Slavinsky, a Pole, saved Rebecca's life. No, not only Rebecca's, all the Silvermans. Oh, my God, Rachel, you are one of the nicest, most intelligent women I know. How can you be so prejudiced? Give your woman's intuition a rest. It's the Sabbath."

"No, the Sabbath's over. Look at the time. How about a cup of tea?"

"Fine, just make sure a Polish clerk didn't sell it to you."

"I don't need any of your sarcasm," she pouts as she stalks into the kitchen.

While I watch her put the kettle on the stove I think about her comments. Although I have humorously dismissed her reservations about Isaac, I know from experience that her first impressions of people are usually correct. I think the young man is intelligent, articulate and decisive, but, I, too, had felt that Isaac's attitude had been – well, I can't quite define it – but …

As Rachel prepares my tea, I make a mental note to look up Isaac's scholastic records as soon as our vacation is over. I'm not going to allow her vague apprehensions deprive our Air Force of a brilliant jet fighter pilot to fly one of the French Mystere jets we just secretly obtained.

Prime Minister Ben Gurion and several of our colleagues in the Israel Defense Force just informed me that they are beginning negotiations with France about acquiring more Mystere jets for our Air Force. Jets are useless if we do not have trained pilots to fly them.

I'm sure, despite my wife's misgivings, that Isaac will make an ideal fighter pilot. If the young man's record is as excellent as I think it should be, as soon as he finishes basic training I will expedite his entry into our flight-training program.

Isaac Ben Abraham

THE RUINS OF ASHKELON

JUNE 1956

Early Sunday morning Rebecca and I wander amid the burned ruins of the Canaanite, Philistine, Roman, Moslem, and Christian settlements in Ashkelon. These artifacts are all that is left of the many civilizations that conquered this little town. Today, at least, the Mediterranean shore is peaceful. As we enter the ancient site we startle a large flock of crows who angrily sound an alarm and whirl furiously around us in defense of their nesting places in the ancient ruins.

"What a cawcawphony," Rebecca smiles as she covers her ears.

I decide to humor her by laughing at her weak joke, but then I grab her arm and gaze in awe at a white mud brick wall surrounded on both sides by twenty foot tall towers. "Look at this gateway. It must be at least eight feet wide."

"Just wide enough for a chariot to pass through, wouldn't you say?" Rebecca asks. "I heard that an archaeologist recently found a silver calf in a little shrine at the end of this roadway. It must have been worshipped by the Canaanites."

"But look at this. This is really amazing. A statue of Nike is next to a statue of Isis!"

"What's so amazing about that?"

"Don't you see? Nike was a Greek goddess and Isis was worshipped by the Egyptians."

"So?"

"That means that people of both religions worshipped in the same temple. Or, at the very least, both peoples were extremely tolerant of each other. Can you see Muslims and Jews worshipping in the same temple today?"

"Only God could make them do that, and He is strangely silent."

"And yet," I counter, "Muslims and Jews both claim Abraham as their common ancestor. And both claim to worship the one true God. In fact, they probably have more beliefs in common than the ancient Greeks and Egyptians did."

"Maybe so," Rebecca says, "but the Greeks ruled the Egyptians and might have adopted many of their religious beliefs and worshipped some of their gods. In fact, I think Cleopatra was Greek. Anyhow, look at poor Nike. She's lost her head. Some goddess of victory."

"And Isis has lost not only her head but her arms as well. But what is that?" I ask pointing to an area on our left.

"Where?"

"It looks like a cemetery of some sort. But not for people."

"I can't believe this," she says. Look at the engravings on the tombs. This is a sacred cemetery for dogs!"

"Who would be so concerned about dogs?" I ask her in wonderment. *These people must have been idiots. Dogs are unclean and no Muslim would give them an honorable burial. How stupid were these ancient people?*

Rebecca crouches down on the ground to scrutinize the graves more carefully.

"The pictures on the tombstones are of Canaan hounds," she says. "We used to have one. He was my father's favorite. When he thought my mother wasn't looking, he would feed the dog her pot roast. Hannah and I would laugh because my mother would feed the dog pot roast when she thought my father wasn't looking. The dog was a master of conniving. He knew how to plead with the most soulful eyes at either one when the other wasn't looking. Neither could resist his soulful look and the hopeful way he wagged his tail whenever he smelled my mother's cooking. He was so good at it that we called him Beggar. He became the most conniving and best-loved member of our family."

"Do you still have him?"

"No, Beggar got old and had severe arthritis. The vet said he had hip dysplasia, which made it difficult for him to walk. At any rate, one day he was in such pain that my father took him to an animal clinic for some medication. We were shocked to see my father come home an hour later with tears running down his cheeks and Beggar's dead body in his arms. The vet who examined Beggar said that the dog's pain was untreatable, and the kindest act would be to put him out of his misery. Papa assured us that he cradled Beggar in his arms while the vet gave him a lethal injection and our dog died peacefully before the doctor had even withdrawn the needle.

"We buried him under the plum tree in our backyard. Every time I look at the tree I think about Beggar, his deep, beseeching eyes, his great faithful heart, and his perpetually wagging tail. Hannah and I used to think that my father loved that dog more than he loved us."

To my amazement I see that she has tears in her eyes. "You were jealous of a dog?"

"No, actually, we loved him very much. Do you know why?"

"Why?"

"He loved us. It's impossible not to love someone who loves you."

"And you still cry over him?"

"Isaac, I can't stop loving someone because he died."

"He wasn't a person; he was a dog! How could these people have built such a vast cemetery for dogs? It's incredible."

"Some dogs are better than some people. Do you know that without dogs, the Canaanites might have had worse famines? This cemetery predates the time of Abraham and those people probably used Canaan dogs to hunt gazelles and deer. Men hunting such swift animals on foot armed with only spears and arrows would be at a tremendous disadvantage without these dogs. Maybe if Esau had used a dog to go hunting he wouldn't have come back empty handed and lost his birthright to Jacob."

"Who's Jacob?"

"JACOB IN THE BIBLE. You're named after his father, idiot." She punches me in the stomach.

"Ouch. I forgot. I'm sorry; I'm just not that fond of dogs and I wasn't thinking about the bible. All I'm thinking about is that there must be 1500 tombstones here, at least. Now all that remains of this civilization has gone to the dogs."

Mental note: find a Hebrew Bible and review everything about Isaac, Jacob, and Esau before I make another faux pas. First that idiot with the donkey in B'nai Berak, and now Rebecca and dogs. Not knowing how these Jews feel about animals will blow my cover faster than anything else. What a people!

Rebecca doesn't seem too perturbed by the fact that I didn't know whom she's talking about. She wanders off and gazes at more tombstone engravings.

"Don't be so cynical. They may have buried their dogs, but Ashkelon was home to many great civilizations. By the way do you know what Canaan means?"

"What?" I ask to humor her. That, at least, I know. But, I'd better play dumb after my last gaffe.

"It means Purple. Possibly, the Philistines came to Ashkelon in search of a shellfish which gave off a substance that allowed them to create the color purple. But they hunted the shellfish to extinction. We think the shekel, our unit of money, gave Ashkelon its name because everyone brought shekels to this place to buy and trade here."

I see something shiny on the ground and pick it up. "This is a coin of some sort. There are sheaves of wheat on one side and a donkey sitting beside a goddess of the fields on the other side."

"Can you make out a date?"

"No, but I'd love to have a magnifying glass and try to make out the inscription. It must be written in Latin. Here, Rebecca, put your scarf on this stone."

Mystified, she lays her white scarf on the rock. I place the ancient coin on the scarf and photograph it. Then I take the scarf and twist it tightly so I can pass it through the large hole at the top of the coin. I walk over to Rebecca and carefully tie the scarf around her neck so that the coin hangs in the little hollow above her collarbone just above her golden Star of David-Christian cross pendant.

"Isaac, this coin has to be very valuable. Perhaps it should be in a museum. You should have it appraised."

"I can't. It's yours."

"But you found it."

"And I put it where it can be displayed most beautifully."

"Are you making a pass at me?"

"Absolutely!"

We both burst out laughing. This is the most relaxing moment I've had all week.

I put my arm around her and together we walk through the relics left by numerous ancient civilizations. I pause by an enormous white marble urn standing on a wide base which is placed on still another, even wider, base. "Look at the intricate carvings of flowers on this vase," I marvel.

I think to myself, *Idiot, you should be quizzing her about her uncle and brother's activities instead of discussing carved flowers on old ruins.*

""That's not a vase; that's an urn," Rebecca smiles.

"What's the difference?"

"A vase costs just a few shekels. An urn must be discovered by an archaeologist, and a young scholar must write an article about it in *National Geographic*," says Rebecca.

"Are you making fun of me?"

"Absolutely!"

"There must have been a giant wall here at one time that surrounded the city," I observe.

"The wall was really useless. First, Nebuchadnezzar burned the city to the ground and took both the Philistines and Hebrew tribes back to Babylon as slaves. And speaking of Cleopatra..."

"The sexy Greek-Egyptian queen," I laugh.

"Her brother exiled her and she gathered together an army in Ashkelon to try to win her kingdom back."

"Did she?"

"No, Antony arrived and fought her battles for her."

"They both lost and died," I remind her.

"Yes, they both lost. Isn't that what usually happens? Some nations win, more lose, and those who love each other die. A thousand years later," Rebecca continues, "the Muslims lived here and built 53 towers to defend Ashkelon from the crusaders. My father keeps calling this place 'Migdal Ashkelon.'"

"The Towers of Ashkelon."

"Right, despite the towers, Richard the Lion Heart defeated the Muslims and Saladin, the great Muslim sheik, burned Ashkelon to the ground rather than let the Christians conquer it. Through the centuries it was really little more than a small village until 1948."

I look at her sunlit face and feel a sudden shiver run through me. I am not doing my job. Instead I am slowly being enthralled by an Israeli girl. *I want to kiss her beautiful face, to hold her hand, to delight in her presence, to make love to her body and also find out her uncle's and brother's military secrets. If I do any of these things I betray her. If I don't, I betray my country.*

Delilah! Did she and Samson walk in this very place? Did he court her here because she captivated him? Did she become his wife because she loved him? Or was she persuaded to marry a man she did not love because her rulers and priests told her that she could use her charms to help them destroy their superhuman brute of an enemy? He did many terrible things to her people, but perhaps the worst one was when he torched their fields of grain. Infernal anger produced an infernal famine.

Did she really love Samson or was she involved in a conspiracy to disarm an enemy of her people? Didn't he realize that he was marrying an intractable foe? Could a man who was the champion and judge of his people be so naïve? I'm sure he didn't lose his strength because Delilah cut his hair. He must have lost it when he saw that Delilah, the woman he loved, had betrayed him. I remember a poem by Robert Frost that my English teacher at Sandhurst made our class memorize:

> *Ah, when to the heart of man*
> *Was it ever less than a treason*
> *To go with the drift of things,*
> *To yield with grace to reason,*
> *And bow and accept the end*
> *Of a love or a season?*

Suddenly Rebecca snaps me out of my reverie. "Isaac, it's getting late and it's getting hot. Do you want to go to the beach now and come back again early tomorrow morning? David and Hannah and her dance group will probably be waiting for us."

"Just one more picture. Stand next to this thousand-shekel urn and let me take a photo of you."

"Why don't you just take a snapshot of the urn?"

"Because if you stand beside it, viewers will have a better idea of its size. They will see that it is at least six feet taller than you are and they will be awed by its scale."

"And you will also have another picture of me."

"Can't fool you. You saw right through my plan."

"I knew as soon as I saw you that you were a devious man."

"Who, me? I'm as honest as they come. Stand on this side; there's too much sun where you are. Its light will over expose the shot."

She moves to the left side of the huge, ancient urn and drapes herself seductively against it.

"Okay, that photo is for me. Now give me a suitable pose for a serious, scholarly article."

She stands next to the urn in a relaxed, but serious manner. "That's it. That's great." I snap the picture and then marvel at how beautiful she looks next to the Greek? Philistine? Roman? Hebrew? urn. As she stands there illuminated by the late morning sun, I impulsively embrace her and kiss her on the forehead.

"Come," I whisper, "It's hot. Let's go to the beach."

She smiles invitingly at me, takes my hand and leads me through the gate. We walk slowly toward the ancient beach which slopes down to meet the foam capped, scalloped waves rippling in from the West.

How many relics, how much debris, how many peoples, how many memories, how much conflict, I wonder, *have the waters of the Mediterranean brought to Ashkelon, their final destination?*

Isaac

On the Beach

June 1956

When we arrive at the beach Rebecca stops a few feet from the water's edge. She shades her eyes against the blazing sun, canvasses the small family enclaves that have laid claim to their few feet of sand, and then shrugs her shoulders. "This is where we're supposed to meet David and Hannah and all her friends, but I see they haven't arrived yet."

"Good," I say as I wipe the sweat from my forehead. "Then there's time for a swim before they bring the picnic lunch. I'm really hot." I peel off my shirt and shorts which I wore over my bathing suit, and slip out of my sandals.

Rebecca takes off her blouse and shorts and reveals a bathing suit which enhances her slim, dancer's body. No Muslim girl would wear a suit like that in public.

"Race you," she calls as she runs toward the foaming waves.

I run after her and together we plunge into the refreshingly cool water.

"This is great. How do Hannah and her crew dance under the burning sun on the hot sand?" I shout over the roar of the waves.

"Oh, they'll wait until late this afternoon. First, everyone eats, and then they'll go for a swim. After a while, someone will play an accordion or a guitar while we all sing some folk tunes. Around 4 or so, one of them will begin to play a drum and a few will start to dance. Slowly, everyone joins in, but we do dance in wet bathing suits, otherwise the heat would be suffocating."

"Why don't they dance indoors?"

"It's really hot indoors without air-conditioning in the late afternoon. The burning sun pounds on the roof all day; by evening the dance studio is oven hot. We only dance indoors after October. It's much better here, where we can wear wet bathing suits and jump in the water whenever we feel the need, trust me, Isaac."

"Rebecca, I do trust you. In fact, I think I do more than trust you."

Suddenly, she staggers against me as a huge wave rolls over us.

I hold her securely and then kiss her tenderly on the lips. I can feel her body against mine and I feel her wet, hard nipples pressing against my chest. Her long, black hair, salty with the sea spray, blows against my face as she passionately returns my kiss. I think, *What in hell am I doing to this girl? What am I doing for Egypt? Betrayal is a two-edged sword. It is morally exhausting and immorally demanding. Traitors are always unfaithful to the trusting. Always faithful to a code that demands duplicity.*

Suddenly she whispers, "I see my sister and brothers coming down the beach."

I immediately let go of her and start to walk out of the water toward them. "Do you think they saw us?"

"And what if they did? Hannah teased me all night about you. Now, at least, she won't ask me endlessly if you finally kissed me. And David thinks anyone who is going to be a jet fighter pilot will be one of the saviors of this country. They would think worse of me if you didn't kiss me."

I am amazed. If she were a proper Muslim girl, her brothers would kill both her and any boy who kissed her on a date, let alone the first one. Here they applaud it! What a culture.

"I hope you're hungry," calls Hannah. "We brought roast chicken, vegetable salad, couscous, watermelon, bananas, bread, cake, and cold drinks. And Aaron is coming with his guitar, Simon is bringing his accordion, and I think Ruben will bring his tambourine and his little Arab drum."

"Did you prepare all this food this morning?" I ask in amazement.

"My mother made the salad and my aunt made the couscous. I made the rest."

"You'll make someone a good wife one day," I say and instantly receive the glare of all glares.

Hannah erupts. Mount Vesuvius in its most violent eruption is less fierce than a furious Hannah. "I hope my husband will want more from a wife than a good meal," she spouts. "I do not intend to spend my life in the kitchen with a bunch of children. I will dance on the stage and everyone will admire me."

Gracefully, she pirouettes across the sand and I have to admit that she is an excellent dancer. Against my will, I begin to applaud and David, much to Hannah's surprise and delight, joins in. All the other people, who are lounging on beach chairs or towels, clap enthusiastically as well, but Rebecca laughs and calls out, "If you're done showing off, Hannah, come help unpack the lunch. I'm starved."

As she spreads a blanket on the sand and begins to unpack the food, about ten young men and women, some carrying musical instruments, approach us. David introduces each one in turn to me, and then the entire group sits down companionably on the blanket and eagerly begins to eat. I make an effort to laugh and joke with the newcomers, who act as though I am their life-long friend. I suppose that I am accepted so quickly into their intimate group because everyone tacitly believes I am Rebecca's boyfriend, and I can see that they all respect her immensely. When the young man named Aaron begins to play his guitar I am relieved no one notices that I don't know the words to the songs they sing.

Damn, this is something else intelligence has to brief us on. I hope they don't start talking about their favorite soccer or basketball players.

I resolve to start reading the sport pages of the daily newspaper and buy a Hebrew folk song book immediately.

Intensely agitated, I am excruciatingly aware of the precarious position I will be in if my true identity is discovered. Most importantly, Egypt will be vulnerable if I cannot find out when and where the Israelis will attack.

Why do I give a damn if I betray Rebecca? That's my job, my duty, my obligation to my family, to my country. I've only known this girl, this ISRAELI girl for a few days. It's her eyes; it's those large, dark eyes that are sad, even when she's smiling.

Desperate to find out if the young men will tell me anything worthwhile about their military plans, I turn toward David, when suddenly Hannah calls, "Look who's coming down the beach. It's Danny back from Jerusalem. Maybe I can show him how a Philistinian dancing girl would have performed in the temple so he'll give me an extra scene in the play." She wiggles her hips provocatively.

"Hannah! Stop that. You're shameless," yells Simon as he pulls her down on the sand.

"Hi, Danny, how was Mass?" he asks the director, who comes over to us and sits down beside our blanket.

"Fine, once the Jordanian soldiers let me pass through the Mandelbaum Gate, and told me how to find the church. Their directions were so great that I only got lost three times. Don't laugh. No one in the old city speaks English or understands my Hebrew. I finally reached the cathedral only to hear some old priest drone away in Latin in the most boring monotone. I would have fallen asleep if I weren't so thrilled to be in the holy city. I know the Latin prayers by rote, but except for a few words I'm damned if I understand what I'm saying."

"That's okay, Danny, I don't think Christ understood too much Latin either," says David. "But then, conquerors never learn the language of the people they defeat. They insist that the conquered learn the language of their conquerors. That's one of the prices of being vanquished. Look at your own country. How many Americans speak Cherokee or Apache?"

Danny nods, "And the Irish Catholics speak Latin in church and English at home, while our good Gaelic language is slowly dying. My grandmother speaks it eloquently, my parents understand it, and I know barely a few words. But you Israelis have revived your language, which has been dead for 2,000 years."

"The comeback kids, that's us," David says sarcastically.

"I'll bet you checked to see if the stage properties you ordered were delivered this morning before you came here," says Simon.

"The costumes have arrived, and I've arranged for some radio ads. And I found some records of the music from the opera *Samson and Delilah* that I want you to listen to, Hannah."

"Opera? I hate opera. Why do you want me to listen to it?"

"It's the ballet music from the Bacchanal, the orgy scene. I'd like you to listen to it, and then see if you can choreograph a provocative and sexy dance to wake the audience up. Do you think you can do that?"

"She's done it already. You should have seen her a few minutes ago," boasted Simon. "She got a standing ovation from everyone on the entire beach. We should have brought tickets to sell. One look at her gyrating away and we'd have standing room only."

"Simon! You're embarrassing me!" blushes Hannah.

"Are you kidding? He's complimenting you. I think your dance will be the high point of the show. In fact, I'm counting on it," says Danny. "Now I just have to work out all the positions, the lighting, the music, the costumes, set, and prop changes. Can you all be at the theater at nine tomorrow morning?"

"Sure," Rebecca and Hannah reply at once.

Simon and I nod and Simon adds, "I'll tell everyone who's not here to be sure to come early tomorrow."

Rebecca asks, "Do you want to do this tech rehearsal before we all have our lines down perfectly?"

Danny nods soberly, "Look, Friday, I crawled home with my tail between my legs and pulled the covers over my head and said, 'Tomorrow has to be better; why am I putting myself through this? Is it worth all this hard work? What else can possibly go wrong? The actors can't act, they don't even want to do this play and no one will give me a break.' Today I'm trying to be positive and solve fifteen problems before we meet tomorrow. I hope you'll all go home tonight and learn your lines so rehearsal will run much smoother tomorrow than it did last week."

"So why do you put yourself through this agony?" asks Hannah.

"Because on a good day, theater gives me a creative high like nothing else can, but on a bad day, I feel as if I'm in the depths of hell."

"Like Friday," says Hannah.

"Like Friday," Danny says grimly. "If some of the performers don't improve, I'll have to think about sending to Tel Aviv for some semiprofessional actors."

"I'll improve," I say quickly. "Now I know that Samson felt that he was a prisoner of his culture and his religion. He trusted a woman he loved, and she betrayed him. He was a man filled with bitter regrets."

"To know this is important," agrees Danny. "To convey this understanding to an audience is another."

"Look," said Hannah. "He'll do better. Anyhow, let's dance. Danny, do you know any Hebrew folk dances?"

"Who, me? I'm not even Jewish."

"So why did you get involved in this play?"

"Love, betrayal, pride, patriotism, religious fanaticism. And a father who must sadly bury his son in the grave he had purchased for himself. This is fascinating stuff. And after all, John Milton wasn't Jewish either."

"Maybe he wasn't Jewish, but he was blind," Simon notes.

"Didn't think of that," Danny says thoughtfully. "One blind man identifying with another and his problems. You don't have to be Jewish or Samson to feel agony. "Notice the play isn't called *Samson and Delilah*. It's *Samson Agonistes*.

Rebecca says, "You know, *agon* was the Greek word for the struggle actors have in a play. So, agony before the curtain goes up is what we're supposed to feel. Lousy rehearsals mean a great performance."

"Come on Danny, I'll teach you a really simple dance." Hannah pulls him up and leads him over to the group. David, Isaac, Tomer, Zipporah, let's go."

"No, no, I can't dance at all," protests David.

"Me neither, my foot's still not healed enough," I say, relieved to hear that David can't dance.

"Oh, the shame of it all. My brother and my sister's boyfriend can't dance. We'll do a very simple one that six-year-olds learn in their sleep. Aaron, play *"Hine Ma Tov"* very slowly."

As Aaron strums the notes to the ancient song, Rebecca and Hannah lead David, Danny, and me through the simple steps. I pretend to limp a little.

After much laughter and awkwardness we learn the dance well enough to earn Hannah's grudging approval. Then the entire group joins hands with us, and as Aaron picks up the tempo, the circle of dancers whirls enthusiastically on the beach. After a few rounds Simon begins to play a more complicated dance on his accordion and Aaron and Ruben accompany him on their instruments. David, Danny, and I cannot possibly manage the intricate steps, and we drop out of the group. As we sit on the sand I have to admire how the accomplished dancers leap with great agility and grace to the trio's music.

"That's a beautiful melody. What's its name?" asks Danny.

"Shir LaShalom, Song of Peace," replies Simon.

My enemies are dancing peacefully while my grandparents lost their home.

I note that while Hannah is the most accomplished dancer in the group, Rebecca is more graceful than her younger sister. Although I don't want to tear my eyes away from her lithesome body I turn to David and casually ask, "How long is your leave from your unit?"

"Simon and I are on a furlough for a few weeks. It's nice to watch him patrol Hannah instead of Jerusalem."

"It must be more dangerous to watch Hannah," says Danny. "Israel already controls Jerusalem. No one controls Hannah."

"We only control the new city of Jerusalem," says David bitterly. "The old city which contains the most sacred monument of our religion, the Temple Mount, is in Arab hands. They won't let us worship where King Solomon built and King Herod rebuilt the great temple which housed our Holy of Holies, the Ark of the Covenant which contained the original Ten Commandments carved in stone. The Arabs have built a huge mosque on the same spot where King Solomon's temple was, covered its roof in gold leaf, and refuse to let any Israeli go near it."

"So build a nicer temple in the new part of the city. Why cling to the past? And what's so special about that spot?" asks Danny.

"You American Christians don't understand," David replies. "You don't have thousands of years of history. Our past is our present and decides our future. The Temple Mount is the spot where God commanded Abraham to sacrifice his son, Isaac. Since Abraham was willing to obey God without question on that site, it serves as the symbolic place of man's total obedience to God's will. We can only rebuild the temple there, on its original foundation."

"If the Muslims knew this site was so sacred to the Jews," muses Danny, "they were really quite offensive when they built the mosque there."

"Not at all," I say quickly. "The Muslims don't think Abraham was going to sacrifice Isaac. They believe his oldest son, Ishmael, who founded the Arab nation, was the sacrificial offering."

"What? I don't believe that," says Danny. "The Bible goes into great detail how Abraham was about to kill the boy until he saw a ram caught by the horns in a shrub and an angel told the distraught father to sacrifice it instead of Isaac."

"Yeah, that's what the Jews and Christians believe. But why would Abraham sacrifice Isaac, the longed-for son of his beautiful wife, Sarah? Why not offer up the first-born son of an Egyptian servant?

Suddenly, I feel David and Simon looking strangely at me. I better say something fast. I am such an idiot.

Quickly, I offer, "The only part of the story that the Jews and Muslims agree upon is the place where the sacrifice of the son was supposed to take place. And the Muslims forbid the Israelis to come near the Temple site where they think Ishmael was to be offered up to Allah. They also think that was the spot where Mohammed ascended to heaven."

"Now, we Christians have the opposite problem," Danny says.

He has no idea how grateful I am that he changes the conversation. Why did I ever say anything?

"We know that Christ was crucified on Calvary, but we disagree where the spot was. The Catholics and Greek Orthodox have erected the Church of the Holy Sepulcher on one site, but the Protestants say Jesus died in another place near a garden tomb."

"But," David says, "neither group denies access to the other."

"No," agrees Danny. "But I just learned the most ironic definition of the word "Jerusalem" today at Mass. Someone told me it means "City of Peace" in Hebrew and yet it is the place where God asked that sons, either his son Jesus, or Abraham's son Isaac, be killed. And how many wars have been waged over it! Come to think of it, I read in an article once by William Sloane Coffin..."

"Coffin! What a morbid name. Who is he?" asks David.

"He preaches at very prominent churches in America and he's the official chaplain at Yale University. Anyhow, Coffin said that Jerusalem, the city of peace, is really a city of God-sanctioned violence. From what I see it's a place where people love to hate.

"After the service I walked the Stations of the Cross. As I retraced His steps, I realized why Christ died. The Romans worshipped War, the great God which unified their empire. His angels were Power, Greed, and Cruelty. Racism and Religion always were and always will be His ammunition that molded and molds his slaves into His vengeful service. Love, Kindness, and Compassion served as the War God's enemies. They are aberrations which seldom appear in mankind. Although they are the saving graces that allow societies and civilizations to exist, they must be extinguished or the War God will starve.

"To gratify their Lord, His chief angels serve Samsonic deaths as dessert."

"What in Hell are you talking about?" asks David.

"That's when, in order to kill large numbers of your enemy, you must kill yourself."

"Kill yourself? Who's crazy enough to do that?" David starts to scoop a little hole in the sand with his fingers.

"Remember, Samson was brought into the temple of the Philistines on one of their religious holidays. Even though he couldn't see, he was no longer blinded by his love for Delilah."

"Smart guy," says Simon.

"You should talk. Hannah can make you do anything she wants."

Before Simon has a chance to protest, Danny continues, "Samson asked a boy to place him between the two pillars that supported the roof of the temple. As the Philistines taunted the man who was once their greatest enemy, he knocked the pillars down.

"The roof collapsed and he crushed not only himself, but more Philistines than he had killed during his entire lifetime. Thus, if anyone dies in such a way he wins a Samsonic victory over his enemies.

"When Samson hated the Philistines he nourished the God of War, but loving Delilah provided this God with an all devouring feast. Maybe I want to defeat Him by putting on this play."

All three of us sit in silence for a while, each alone in our thoughts.

Suddenly, David asks softly, "What is that out there?"

When he repeats his question in a louder and somewhat tenser voice, I reluctantly look away from the dancing figure of Rebecca and ask, "What are you looking at?"

Danny stands up and shades his eyes to get a better look. He says, "It looks like a rubber boat that's rapidly coming toward us. It must have an attached outboard motor to approach so quickly."

Suddenly shots ring out and I see that a machine gun, positioned in the front of the boat, is aimed straight at us.

"Everyone, get down," David yells as he runs towards his sisters and brother and throws them under him in back of a small sand dune. He tries to shelter them with his body as bullets bombard the beach. Lethal explosions of sand erupt at our feet as Simon and

I run with the other dancers. We manage to lie down behind the dune which offers about three feet of protection, but protection nevertheless.

Simon yells at Danny who is staring bewilderingly at the raft to run for cover, but before the director reaches the tiny rise of sand, he is hit repeatedly with bullets. His gut-wrenching scream of "JESUS" reverberates across the beach as he staggers towards us. Years later I will still hear that scream in my dreams.

As quickly as it became visible, the boat turns and heads toward Gaza. The moment it disappears everyone runs towards Danny's mutilated body. Blood is pouring from his stomach, neck, and thighs. David cradles the director's sightless head in his arms as Simon feels desperately for a pulse. I put my arm around Rebecca, who is sobbing hysterically, and murmur softly to Simon, "Don't bother. He's with his Christ now in the New Jerusalem."

Ishmael

MISSION ACCOMPLISHED

OCTOBER 1956

I grip the wheel tightly as my mind races over the events of the last months. The day after the massacre at the beach the cast of *Samson Agonistes* held a memorial ceremony at the airport when Danny O'Halloran's casket was shipped back to his family in the United States. The cast unanimously agreed that the play would not go on with a substitute director.

Rebecca, and especially Hannah, along with Simon and David, were bent on revenge, and only wanted to concentrate on their upcoming military duties. I learned both sisters had just been notified that they were about to be inducted into the infantry attached to a medical unit. Omar and I concluded that any information I could glean from the young people's conversations about the army's mobilization plans would be valuable.

Omar instructed me to continue to court Rebecca and learn from her all I could about David's paratroop unit and any information about the Israeli Air Force from her uncle who had taken an immense liking to me.

I did not do this willingly because I felt myself falling more and more in love with her.

> To love unloved is a curse.
> To love and be loved in return by someone you dare
>   not love is Hell.
> To betray the enemy is right; it is proper; it is retribu-
>   tion of the highest order.

To be treacherous to Rebecca is destroying my soul.

To be true to her will destroy my parents, my people, my country.

Yesterday afternoon Omar met me at our usual daily rendezvous and was more tense than normal. "General Ben Dassan, Rebecca's uncle, has been making inquiries about you. He wants to know whether you can go to flight training school at Tel Nuf after basic training."

"How do you know?"

"We have a mole in the Kiryah, the Israeli intelligence agency, who knows about all our activities here and the assignment of every one of our agents. When he saw the inquiry about you he forwarded to the general our prepared dossier about your sterling achievements at Sandhurst as the greatest Israeli student ever to attend the Academy."

"I'm sure you erased my horrendous grades in mathematics."

"We lied like hell. The report stated you earned a first in every course. But this inquiry made us decide that your usefulness to us is over here. We have just one last job for you. Say goodbye today to Rebecca and any other friends you've made. Tell them you've finished your article on the ruins of Ashkelon for National Geographic and the doctor has cleared you for army duty. Tell them you're going to begin basic training immediately. We don't want them wondering about your whereabouts for the next few days. Then, move out of your apartment and go to Tel Aviv."

"Tel Aviv?"

"In the evening go to the Habimah Theater. Do you know where it is? Good. At the box office ask for a ticket reserved for Rami Jacobs."

"Who's that?"

"You. Get there at least thirty minutes before the show begins so the building should be fairly empty. Israelis always come late to the theater. Your seat will be on the aisle in the last row of the balcony. Our man will be sitting in the seat next to yours.

"When you give him the password he will hand you an envelope which contains vital information which must be conveyed to Cairo immediately. Since most of the audience, especially those who have seats in the balcony, will have not arrived yet, you should arouse no suspicion if you leave soon after you receive the documents. Drive immediately to our army headquarters in Gaza, where I will be waiting for you and the envelope. If all goes according to plan we should meet between eleven p.m. and midnight."

"May I ask what is in the envelope?"

"Our mole in Israeli Intelligence learned from a spy we have in Beirut, whom we suspect is really a double agent for Russia, some very sensitive information he has copied. It details an Israeli plan to attack the Suez Canal in conjunction with Britain and France. Oh, and you might find this amusing. The Israeli name for this attack is 'Hand of Samson.'"

"Amusing, no. Ironic, yes. And the password is...?"

"All Palestine from the Mediterranean Sea to the Jordan River is ours!"

"Shouldn't the password be something less inflammatory to an Israeli in case the man sitting next to me isn't a mole but a Jew?"

"We've already bought the tickets for both of you, so I don't think there is any chance anyone else would be sitting beside you, but what do you have in mind?"

"How about something I learned in physics which would be quite appropriate in this situation?"

"And that is?"

"The powers of adhesion are determined by group particle affinity."

"Shit, Ishmael, stop pretending to be an intellectual college bastard! I don't even know what that means, and there's no damn way I could remember it long enough to transmit it to our man in the Kiryah."

For the first time that afternoon I laughed out loud.

"Well," says Omar dryly, "when you're done laughing at me, college boy, get going. When we rendezvous in Gaza we'll fly together with this document to Cairo. Then, I hear headquarters has a very interesting assignment for you in London."

"London!"

"Yes, it's vital that you obtain information for us regarding English involvement in Egyptian internal affairs. We suspect that the British want to assassinate Nasser. You will become George Halaby, a student at the London School of Economics, and begin your covert operations at once."

"So my college experience is worthwhile after all."

"Don't get so cocky. We could just as easily make your cover that of an uneducated cockney waiter and plant you in 10 Downing Street. In fact, that's what I wanted Intelligence to do, but I was voted down. Someone there likes brash university students – the morons!"

As we say goodbye to each other, I realize that this is the last humorous moment I will ever have in Israel. Thanks to our spy in Beirut, the unified cycle of duplicity is complete.

Treason can be a blessing and a curse.

The full moon glares threateningly at me as I drive to Tel Aviv.

The ocean roars ominously.

The plans are waiting for me to deliver to Egyptian intelligence.

I will never see Rebecca again.

As I drive toward Tel Aviv through the early evening traffic I imagine that Rebecca's breasts are under my hands instead of the steering wheel. I ache with longing to feel not only her breasts, but also her entire body under mine. Last night when I took her to the beach and told her I was leaving the next day for basic training, she delicately took my hand in hers and I could sense her subdued, worried concern. As the waves crashed and receded upon the shore, I drew her down to the sand and kissed her eyes, her mouth, and then caressed her throat with my tongue. Slowly I unbuttoned her blouse and cupped first one breast, then the other in my hand. I took each firm, red nipple into my mouth and savored its sweetness. Then, hesitatingly, because I feared that she would stop me, I unzipped her jeans and slid them down to her thighs. I nuzzled her slim, smooth stomach and licked the insides of her navel. To my astonishment and delight, she slowly slipped out of her jeans and then clasped me closely to her in a tight embrace.

"This is not goodbye," she whispered. "This is hello. While you are in basic training, I want you to know what you have waiting here for you in Ashkelon."

Wordlessly, I stroked her hair and then, feeling an unconquerable rush of desire flood through me, I began to caress her entire body again with my tongue. As I neared her mound of Venus she parted her thighs and I saw that she was uncircumcised.

"You're not?"

"I'm not what?"

Khara, I almost asked her why she's not circumcised. What a way to blow my cover! Remember, you idiot, the Jews, like the English, don't circumcise their women.

And then I silently gave thanks to all the English girls who had taught me how to arouse an uncircumcised woman.

"Rebecca," I stammered, "What I meant to ask is…. How do I put it? Are you a virgin?

"Is my inexperience that obvious?"

"Yes. Be serious now. Are you sure you want to give your virginity to me?

"Isaac, I love you."

"What if I don't come back?"

"Why wouldn't you come back?"

"How can you ask that? Look what happened to Danny O'Halloran."

"Then I can't think of a better reason to make love to you."

Soberly, I looked into her dark eyes and what I saw there made me realize that no one would ever love me as much as Rebecca did.

I kissed her until I could feel the sexual tension pulsing in her aroused body. Then, as gently as I could, I entered her and made love to her for both the first time and the last time in my life.

She is the Palestine of my desires. The Jerusalem I will conquer.

When I tenderly withdrew from her I rested my head on her shoulder and softly stroked her hair. "I brought you here tonight to tell you I don't know when I'll see you again. Basic training is demanding, and I don't know when I'll have my first leave."

"War is in the air. David has returned to his unit. Tanks have been going from Jerusalem to the Jordanian border for two days now," she says.

"Simon is in the same company, isn't he?"

"They enlisted together. You know, they've been friends since they were five years old. And they may be even closer soon."

"You think he may become your brother-in-law?"

"Hannah and he have become almost inseparable. In fact, they're out together somewhere tonight, too."

"They're probably also saying goodbye to each other."

"But only for a few days. David and Simon will be home by the weekend. Israel can't afford a long campaign against Jordan. Anyhow, they are in a paratroop unit and so far, only tanks are going to the border.

"You, David, and Simon must come back. You are the three men who mean the most to me. Never ever say you don't know when you'll see me again."

I sat up and stared out to sea for a few moments. Then I turned with a wry smile and said,

> The sea is calm tonight
> The tide lies full
> The moon lies fair

"Do you know that poem?"

"No, what is it?"

"It's called 'Dover Beach' by Matthew Arnold. I had to learn it in one of my English Literature classes. And the ending seems so perfect for tonight, for us, for this scene, for Israel, and for the Middle East."

"Do you still remember it?"

Ah love, let us be true
To one another! For the world, which seems
To lie before us like a land of dreams,
So various, so beautiful, so new,
Hath really neither joy, nor love, nor light,
Not certitude, nor peace, nor help for pain
And we are here as on a darkling plain
Swept with confused alarms of struggle and flight
Where ignorant armies clash by night.

"Ignorant armies?" asked Rebecca.

"Ignorant armies! Ignorant generals! Ignorant politicians!"

I turned from the sea to look at Rebecca. I saw in her the embodiment of everything serene, humane, gracious, and lovely. Desperate because I know I cannot ever see her again and guilt-ridden because of my necessary duplicity, I embrace her. As I do I notice that the sand underneath the area where she is sitting is tinged with blood. Quickly, I try to cover it.

"Isaac, it's all right. The tide will come in soon and wash it away."

"We don't need to leave any evidence of what we did here tonight," I say as I stand up and help her rise beside me.

As we walk slowly off the beach under the light of the full moon I thought, *How much more blood will flow because of me, because of her, because of the cryptic covenant Israel has made with its God, because my people are exiled from this land, because throughout its history everyone desired it passionately, and no one held it peacefully for any length of time?*

Oh Jerusalem, you city of men's desiring.

You cause of wars.

Diana, The Goddess of the Moon

DIES IRAE

OCTOBER 1956

The moon shines brilliantly on the road leading from Ashkelon to Tel Aviv. Her iridescent light caresses the Mediterranean Sea that borders the highway and glimmers in the headlights of Ishmael's car. But now her smile becomes ominous when she realizes where the tense young man is going. Last night she observed how he transformed the innocent, young Rebecca into an adoring, mature woman. As she rose above the sea's horizon she beamed benevolently at them while they made passionate love on the beach. The lunar deity was so moved by their tender feelings for each other that she asked her pagan sister, Palés, the donkey goddess of fertility, to bless their union with a son. Then, she watched sadly as Rebecca said a tearful goodbye to the handsome young man who told her he must report to basic training. The sentimental moon adores lovers, but tonight, when she finally realizes his true destination and the extent of his treachery, she robes herself in thick black clouds. The stars fade into the smoky firmament and darkness envelops all the earth.

Waves of war roar up the beach that edge his route toward Tel Aviv.

David Ben Gurion
THE PROTOCOL OF SÈVRES
OCTOBER 1956

"So, gentlemen, Israel is to be a prostitute performing services for France and England," I state grimly to the men facing me. Shimon Perez, my Director General of Defense, and Moshe Dayan, the Israeli Defense Forces Chief of Staff, nod in agreement at my bold statement.

I pull no punches. Not me. I know what France and England want. Sir Anthony Eden, the noble ass of England, thinks the Egyptian president, Gamal Abdel Nasser, is as malevolent as Adolf Hitler. That strutting liar of a French peacock, Guy Mollet, is upset that Nasser nationalized (diplomatic doubletalk for "stole") the Suez Canal in July. After all, these two countries received more than three-quarters of a million dollars a day in fees. Who cares that the canal is built on Egyptian soil? To the builders belong the tolls.

"You two countries think the Egyptians gypped you. Now, you need an excuse to attack Egypt, and you can't find a reason to justify any such attack. Diplomacy with Nasser is getting you nowhere. So you want us to do your dirty work for you. Of course, when we get too close to the Suez Canal, you will appeal to the United Nations and have the pretext to separate us from the Egyptians to protect the canal. Also, the British prime minister feels he is under no obligation to stop Israelis from attacking Egyptians."

I glare at the assembled diplomats facing me, "Sir Anthony wants us to be the prostitute and he hopes for an immaculate intervention."

Guy Mollet, French Prime Minister, Christian Pineau, French Foreign Affairs Minister, Maurice Bourges-Maunoury, French Minister of Defense, Selwyn Lloyd, British Under Secretary of State, and Patrick Dean, Assistant Under-Secretary of the British Foreign Office, grin at my blunt but accurate assessment of the situation.

And I am making sure that the secretary of our delegation, Colonel Mordechai Bar-On, is taking copious notes of our entire three-day conference here in this secluded villa. I want this recorded so that Israel will be compensated for whoring herself to these Western powers. The English want to use us to remove Nasser from power and give Jordan to Iraq while France believes that Nasser is a dangerous new dictator, especially since he supports the Algerian rebels. They think only military action will allow them to regain the canal and knock Nasser off his perch.

The French not only want the canal back, but they are concerned that they may lose their colony in Algeria. If Nasser is toppled they think that the Algerian rebellion will collapse, since he supports their fight for independence.

I stare intently at each of the diplomats in turn. "You want the whole world to see Israel as the aggressor and perceive England and France as peacemakers and rescuers of the Suez Canal. Gentlemen, I will not lie to the rest of the world and do your dirty work for you!"

"Now, I have a fantastic plan. I know it's fantastic, but it will give each of us what we want. Jordan will never succeed as an independent state and should be divided. Iraq should get the land on the east bank of the Jordan River as a reward for settling the Palestinian refugees there and for making peace with Israel.

The West Bank will be attached to Israel. Lebanon has problems with a large Muslim population in the south. We can solve this problem by having Israel gain all the land in Lebanon up to the Litani River, which would help turn Lebanon into a more compact Christian state.

The Suez Canal area should be given an international status while the Straits of Tiran will come under Israeli control to ensure freedom of navigation. Under these terms we will help you get rid of Nasser and replace him with a pro-Western government."

I can see immediately that the British think my plan is a Zionist dream with no chance of success. They know we Israelis don't trust them. We haven't since they expelled us from England in 1290.

Damn them. Without Jewish money and political influence they never would have been able to build their canal in the first place.

The French, however, will support us in almost every way to get the Suez Canal back and topple Nasser. My staff and I will support these arrogant bastards under these three conditions:

I want to lift Egypt's blockade of the Straits of Tiran and ensure freedom of navigation for Israel to Asia and Southern Africa. I want France to help us build a nuclear reactor in Dimona in the Negev Desert, and finally I want them to help us run an oil pipe line from the new reserves just found in the south of the Sinai Peninsula to Haifa.

I also told the French minister that it would be good to tear the Sinai Peninsula away from Egypt because it did not belong to her; the English stole it from the Turks when they believed that Egypt was in their pocket.

So for three days we scheme, doubt, and manipulate each other. At the end of our meeting, I feel that Israel will become an important ally of the western nations, and our tiny state will be on an equal footing with England and France.

To make sure that our attack is successful, France will give us Mystere Jets painted to look like Israeli planes and naval protection during our invasion into the Sinai. A year later she will provide us with a nuclear reactor, thus we will be the only country in the Middle East with atomic power. With forty million enemies bent on our annihilation, the bomb is the only way to insure our existence.

But I don't trust these ministers, and I insist that these conditions be put in writing. Our secretaries hastily type up the Protocol of Sevres and each of us signs it. At last, Israel will be accepted as an equal ally of the major western powers.

With this written assurance I tell the ministers that the Israel Defense Force will attack Egypt on October 29.[3]

---

3 Sir Anthony Eden was so furious that The Protocol of Sevres was put in writing that he burned it as soon as it was delivered to him while the French minister burned it as soon as the war was over. David Ben Gurion, the Israeli prime minister, however, kept it in his records. The Protocol was published twenty years after Ben Gurion's death. The accounts of this secret meeting were obtained from the web site www.TheProtocolofSevres.com. Much of the dialogue is quoted verbatim from this source.

THE HAND OF SAMSON

OCTOBER 29, 1956

"God is great!" the Arabs yell triumphantly as they kill us. Well, God may be great, but man is murderous.

I am sitting alone, terrifyingly alone, in the belly of a Dakota plane with 29 other scared shitless paratroopers of the Lion Brigade. Our flimsy World War II plane, which should have been put in a museum of military antiquities along with King David's slingshot, is flying in formation with 15 other Dakotas deep into the central Sinai Peninsula to the eastern end of the Mitla Pass just 45 miles from the Suez Canal.

We've been briefed on our mission that the government in its infinite wisdom calls "Hand of Samson." We all know what happened to him.

Everyone who fights is a moral murderer, yet how else can we defend our land?

Everyone needs a home, but the mortgage is truly a death hold. My God, my God, what kind of a banker are you?

Our colonel sits in the center of the belly of the lead plane surrounded by apprehensive yet determined soldiers who are filled with the palpable tension that always precedes an impending battle. Each nervously waits for the command to jump into the backbone of the Sinai. War may be Hell, but the moments before the actual fighting begins are absolutely intolerable.

I nervously readjust the shoulder harness of my parachute and pray, as I always do before each jump, that it will open when I pull the rip cord. Suddenly an eloquent silence reverberates through the aisles as the pilot announces that we are approaching our destination. This stillness communicates an anxiety so overwhelming that I feel I will go mad if I do not break the tension that envelops the plane.

"Simon," I whisper, "The Egyptians won't mount a major defense against us."

"Why not?"

"Because five days ago Israel sent a force of 30 tanks from Jerusalem toward Jordan to create the impression that we are going to mount a major attack against it in retaliation for terrorist actions against frontier towns near the Jordanian border."

"Thirty tanks may be enough if we were only going to fight against Jordan," Simon whispers, "but Iraq has already sent troops there, and Egypt and Syria will send forces, too. Everyone knows that Britain will also support Jordan."

"But my uncle told me we don't intend to attack Jordan, at all. That night, all the tanks came back under the cover of darkness. Then, each morning for the next four mornings, the same tanks drove down the highway in clear sight of the Jordanian and Egyptian spies and every night the 30 tanks with their headlights turned off, came back. So, the Egyptians believe that we have hundreds of tanks there and they also think that all the mobilization their spies saw are preparations for an attack on the Jordanian border."

"Are there no tanks or armies massed on the Jordanian front?" asks Simon.

"None! My uncle told me we are going to the Sinai. The Jordanians can sit on their asses and wait for a battle that will never come."

"Lucky for Jordan. Rotten for Egypt." Simon says wryly.

"It will become even more rotten. I overheard Colonel Goldberg tell the pilot that four of our P-51 Mustang fighters flew to just 12 feet above the ground and cut all the overhead telephone lines in the Sinai with their wings and propellers. Now, Egyptian communications from the Sinai to Egypt are completely cut off."

"And," our colonel who overheard me talking to Simon adds, "we hope the Egyptian war machine will take a long time to move from Jordan to the Sinai, which will give us a chance to deploy near the canal before the United Nations and superpowers react. All we really want to do is openly threaten the Suez Canal, thereby furnishing the French and English the pretext they need to intervene to protect it."

"So," asks Simon, "What do we get out of all this? Use of the canal?"

"Israel doesn't give a damn about the canal. The Straits of Tiran is our Suez. Without this outlet we are forced to sail through the Mediterranean and around Africa to get to India, China, and Japan. I don't care if the English, the French, or the United Nations controls the canal, but if we don't break the Egyptian blockade at Tiran we're prisoners in our own country."

"So why are we here in the middle of the Sinai? Why aren't we going south to the Straits?" asks Simon.

"We're going to prevent the Egyptians from attacking our forces that are already on the way there. Egypt will think we're retaliating for those damned fedayeen raids and fight against us, so our 9th Brigade can advance toward Sharm el Sheikh and break the blockade.

At that moment, the navigator approaches us. "Sir, the pilot says we're directly over our target."

The colonel barks sharply, "Lion Brigade! Parachute out."

Relieved at finally receiving the order to act, I feel the tension drain from me as I quietly rise to stand with the others in a single file by the open hatch. I watch as each man in front of me catapults through the door; when my turn comes I jump into the crystal blue air and drift down into the Sinai's Mitla Pass. As I float through the air a montage of images flashes through my mind. Time seems suspended as I envision the land beneath me, the paratroopers around me, and the battle about to begin. Finally, after an excruciatingly interminable dream of what my life has been and will be, I watch my parachute's loose canvas gracefully metamorphose into an air-filled white mushroom.

In a heartbeat I become a pendant dangled by the gods of gravity, wind, and war.

Suddenly, my feet hit the barren, sand-strewn, rock-bound desert and an intense sense of the reality of the moment literally and figuratively brings me back to earth. I look around for Simon and see that he has landed just 20 feet away from me. We scramble for cover and tensely wait for battle instructions.

As we huddle under a rocky outcropping, I stare at the belligerent desert expanse shimmering in waves of heat and stretching forbiddingly toward the eastern end of the world. "Did you ever wonder, Simon, who your ancestors were and what they did 500, 1000, or even 2,000 years ago?"

"Yeah, that's all I have on my mind at this moment."

"Think about it. Five hundred years ago my family was probably running away from Spain. How long do you think it took them to make their way to Poland? A thousand years ago they were probably hiding from the Crusaders. Two thousand years ago they were probably driven out of Judea by the Romans. It just hit me that maybe three thousand years ago they were fugitives from Egypt crossing this very Sinai desert with Moses. How could so many millions have lived in this barren wasteland for 40 days let alone 40 years? A scorpion can't even survive here."

Simon looks at me incredulously. "We're holed up in a pass. We're target practice for trigger-happy Egyptians and you're wondering if your ancestors were involved in crucial historical migrations! Are you nuts? Forget about great-great-grandpa a zillion generations back dancing around a golden calf and catching hell from Moses, or your relatives a thousand generations ago trying to avoid being burned at the stake by Ferdinand and Isabella. Think about the Egyptian mortars which could be aimed at us tomorrow."

"I'm serious. I always wondered what my ancestors thought and did. What went through their minds when they traveled in this barren desert? It's so dry that my pee evaporates before it hits the ground. I feel as if I've come full circle. Here I am defending my nation again from the Egyptians. Doesn't this shit ever end?"

"No, you're fucking scared. You aren't wondering if your ancestors were among the original members of the 12 tribes. You don't care if they fled west across Europe one step ahead of the Romans or ran east one mile in front of the Crusaders. You're not thinking about how your ancestors survived here; you're wondering if WE will."

"Sure, I'm scared. I'd be an idiot if I weren't. Everyone plans for the future, and I don't know if I have one. But I do have a past. Don't you wonder about yours?"

Simon laughs. "Never, the past is over and done with. Ariel Sharon controls my present, and I don't even know if I control my future. I don't give a shit what my ancestors did. You're as terrified as I am, so you're talking about what happened thousands of years ago so you won't think about how scared you are right now. What all of us are most scared of is letting anyone else know how scared we are."

"All I've been thinking about ever since we parachuted from the plane is I'm fighting for a land that is half desert, half rocks, and contains a dead sea, that God, in his infinite generosity gave us.

"How did Moses forge a culture in this shitty desert?" David continues. "All the Hebrew slaves died here after winning their freedom. And where does that leave us? Fighting against that same country 3,000 years later." David takes off his helmet and wipes the sweat off his forehead. "I wish I were in the Dead Sea right now."

"Moses was a dreamer," muses Simon. "Look where his dreams landed us. Isn't this a perfect setup for a massacre?"

"Maybe Moses will come back, wave his rod over the barren desert, and the Egyptians will disappear."

"It'd be better if he waved a rod over the burning sand and some water appeared. Egyptians we can handle."

Simon hands me my canteen. "Now, have a drink because this miserable desert is going to get hotter before you have a chance to write your memoirs down for your grandchildren to marvel over."

I lift my canteen and tap Simon's with it. "L'Chaim!"

Simon smiles and taps his canteen against mine. "L'Chaim! With Mayim."[4]

After taking a long drink Simon gazes out at the barren, rock-strewn landscape. "You're right. This is some promised land," he says cynically.

"This isn't the promised land. This is the Sinai."

"The Negev is much better? And you don't even have to go to the Negev. Our great founding father, Abraham, settled in such a fertile place that famine swept the land almost as soon as he arrived.

"Half of it is salt water, sand, and rocks. Why didn't He give us Hawaii? Now there's a Promised Land!"

"Then we wouldn't be an independent Jewish nation. We'd be a territory of the United States."

"Don't worry. I'm sure we would fight a war with the U.S. for our independence. We're so smart we might be just dumb enough to win, too."

"Imagine. Would we have to give America foreign aid?"

"Of course. Chicken soup with matzo balls every Friday night."

"No, no. No. We're in Hawaii. Pineapple upside-down cake and surfboards for everyone!"

We drink sparingly from our canteens and hunker down to wait for Ariel Sharon's forces to join ours.

After an interminable wait we receive additional supplies and reinforcements. We are sure that Egyptian intelligence cannot know we are preparing an attack in the Sinai. The element of surprise is our key tactic.

But while the Arabs have the impression that there will be an attack across the Jordanian border, Colonel Ariel Sharon's unit has left Jordan and joined ours. He soon makes a decision that will have a devastating effect upon all of us who are engaged in Operation Hand of Samson.

---

4 L'Chaim is a Hebrew toast which means "To life." "Mayim" is the Hebrew word for "water."

All our commanders are sure that the Egyptians are uncertain about Israel's military intentions. They have no idea that Ishmael has given documents about the meeting at Sevres to Egyptian military intelligence that has caught the attention of their Minister of Defense and Commander-in-Chief, General Abd el Hakim Amer. No Israeli commander knew when Amer learned that the telephone wires in the Sinai had been cut he left Jordan, returned to Egypt, and ordered the Egyptian 2nd Brigade from Suez to deploy in the Mitla Pass.

Simon will later learn when he reads an account of this battle in Chaim Herzog's book *The Arab-Israeli Wars* that Sharon received an intelligence report from an Israeli spy placed inside the Egyptian high command that the enemy force in the pass consisted of only two companies with two mortars and two machine gun platoons. Yet this force, hiding in the caves, was invisible to the Israeli reconnaissance planes.

So while the two armies acted on intelligence from their own espionage operations, jockeyed for positions and devised their military strategies, our Lion Paratroopers prepared for the onslaught.

"Simon, why in Hell are we defending the Mitla Pass and becoming cannon fodder? They aren't posing any danger to our forces that are advancing to Sharm El-Sheikh."

"Simple. Sharon wants to ensure that the Egyptians can't follow him down to Sharm El-Sheikh. He wants the Mitla Pass secured. He feels that if he moves the 202nd Brigade and the Lion Paratroopers south, the enemy in the pass will follow and attack us."

"But that force is purely defensive. They are only there to prevent us from reaching the Suez Canal. If we go into the pass and advance further we'll be in violation of the UN ultimatum to stop eight miles before the Canal."

"You know that. I know that. Sharon knows that. But I think Sharon will convince Moshe Dayan that it is necessary for us to go into the Pass to reconnoiter and to prevent the Egyptians from attacking us while we advance on Sharm El Sheikh."

"And you don't think it's necessary?" I ask.

"No, but what do I know? I just follow orders."

"Ours but to do or die." I shrug.

Simon winces at my sarcastic remark. "No more talk of dying. I can't stand morbid soldiers who make parodies of stupid poems."

I survey the barren, rock-strewn pass. "Fascinating place. Our ancestors wandered through this hell of a desert so we could come back thousands of years later to defend the land they could only dream about."

"You know, those old Hebrews would say not much has changed. We're still fighting the Egyptians."

"Oh, a lot has changed. Now we're not just freed slaves, but Israelis who have a country of our own, a culture of our own, a religion of our own..."

"And a reckless colonel of our own who's leading us into a Pass that's not our own."

"Reckless, shit. David, after this battle is over, the Mitla Pass will be ours."

"Just what I always wanted. Don't stop with the Pass. Maybe, Simon, the whole Sinai will be ours."

"Won't our ancestors be surprised?"

"Yeah, David. But don't you be the one to find them and tell them."

We look at each other and burst out laughing

Two days later we are not laughing. We are still joking though. As bullets whistle through the air Simon asks, "Horrible shots, aren't they? That last bullet missed me by inches."

I tell him, "If you were a little fatter, it would have hit you."

Colonel Ariel Sharon is impatient. Our brigade is holed up at a place called the Parker Memorial. He can't stand that Dayan wants to leave the Israeli Defense Force's elite paratroopers out of the battle. Moshe Dayan, our chief of staff, doesn't want him to go west towards the Suez Canal. Sharon can't sit still. He asks for permission to capture the Mitla Pass. Dayan refuses.

Herzog describes in his account of the battle that when Rehavam Ze'evi, the chief of the Southern Command arrived, Sharon convinced him that it was necessary to send a small patrol into the

Mitla Pass. Sharon was confident there were no Egyptian armies there, so he sent a "beefed-up patrol" of several companies into the area. He didn't know that several Egyptian companies were waiting for us. Simon, who will become an inveterate scholar of the war, will always wonder how the Egyptians knew the Lion paratroop unit was deployed to the Sinai.

Under Sharon's orders, Major Mordechai Gur tells us to advance into the pass.

Our advance is led by a half-track mounted rifle company. A half-track is an ingenious vehicle whose front has the same chassis as a truck with artillery mounted on its hood. The rear is propelled by tank-like caterpillar tracks which allow it to carry heavy loads, personnel, and ride over almost any kind of terrain.

The Egyptians, who are familiar with the Sinai, are hidden in trenches and niches in the cliffs, and pin us down.

Our casualties mount and in a harrowing few minutes many paratroopers are killed. Lethal fire from Hell rains down on us.

I am driving the jeep of the Reserve Commander. Simon is riding in the back of the jeep and is the wireless radio operator. As soon as we enter the Pass we are immediately attacked by the invisible enemy. There seems to be no escape from the murderous hail of bullets from invisible guns.

In the early evening when the fighting becomes desperate and the paratroopers are in danger of total annihilation Simon whispers to me, "I just want to tell you that on our last night in Ashkelon I asked Hannah to marry me."

"What did she say?"

"She said she'd marry me if I promised to do the cooking."

"Sounds just like Hannah. If she does the cooking, the two of you will starve."

We both burst out laughing. I ignore the barrage of bullets and whisper to Simon, "My God, you'll really be part of our family now." I grab Simon and enthusiastically embrace him. Then we fire and dodge, dodge and fire, fire and dodge.

During a pause in the ballistic barrage I look at the forsaken desert. Forget scorpions; not even a cockroach can survive in this wasteland.

I am here because of the collective memories of all my ancestors. I am one with them, and they are one with me.

I am fighting for a homeland that enemies have always tried to keep from us.

No wonder you can't go home again. Those who take it from you won't let you reclaim it.

"David," my commander yells at me, "drive the jeep towards the cliff and draw the Egyptians' fire. Drive quickly and aim as many rounds at them as you can with your machine gun.

"Their soldiers will then shoot at you and reveal their position. Once we know where they are, we'll be able to get the Hell out of here."

I know there isn't any chance of my surviving this order. I remember when Danny told Isaac what a Samsonic death is. Now it's my turn to be Samson. What did I say to Simon yesterday?

> *I am not to question why.*
> *I am but to do or die.*
> *Into the valley of death*
> *The mortar thundered*
> *But I am ordered by my commander*
> *To save the three hundred.*
> *Why does love of land, love of religion, love of family, and love*
> *of friends require people to die so these loves can live?*

I grab Simon's hand for one last time and whisper, "Be a good husband to Hannah."

I cannot look at my commander. He cannot look at me. I start the ignition and begin the last journey of my life.

The Egyptians aim round after round at my Jeep as my machine gun mounted on its hood fires at them. They ignore our paratroopers who are now able to retreat under the cover of darkness. Just as Simon's truck reaches the safety of the Israeli emplacement an

Egyptian bazooka hits my gas tank. The desert quakes and the stone walls of the Mitla Pass reverberate as the huge explosion spews metal shards of my vehicle and fragments of my body into the desert night air. Frozen in place by the sight of the immense fireball in their midst, the Egyptians watch in horror as my flaming death rapidly envelops them.

Simon

AFTER OPERATION HAND OF SAMSON

NOVEMBER 1956

The Lion paratroopers and the 202nd Brigade were saved by David's heroic act. Our commander denied that he ordered David to undertake a suicidal mission and would state that David volunteered. I lost my best friend and learned later that Hannah had also been killed when her Jeep rode over a land mine. The 9th Brigade reached Sharm El-Sheikh and ended the blockade of the Straits of Tiran. Colonel Sharon would be severely criticized for his engagement in the Mitla Pass and the whole operation would be considered unnecessary from a tactical or strategic point of view. Moshe Dayan, Israel's Defense Chief of Staff, endured a great deal of criticism because he didn't bring a court-martial against Sharon.

I should have brought a court-martial against Sharon.

Ironically, since the electorate of Israel suffers fools gladly, Sharon will later be elected prime minister of Israel for his risky strategies. He will participate or be accused of causing several massacres and make mistake after tactical mistake, but none so great as the one that resulted in David's death.

He will spend his last years in a coma caused by a stroke. Ariel Sharon, the Lion of Israel, lies comatose, and David is dead because of this Lion's pride.

Before Sharon suffers his stroke, he will withdraw all Israeli settlers and soldiers from the Gaza Strip, but I predict the hostilities between the Arabs and Jews will last until men land on Mars. Mars, in His infinite capacity as the God of War, will probably ensure that they continue to fight across the universe. Isn't it ironic that Arabs and Israelis greet each other with the word "Peace" which is Salaam in Arabic and Shalom in Hebrew? Both claim one founding ancestor, yet they have one of the most non-peaceful internecine conflicts on earth.

But the war has several beneficial consequences. Israel now has access to the Straits of Tiran and the Suez Canal. Nasser collects its tolls and will construct the High Dam at Aswan to revitalize the Egyptian economy and agriculture.

A year after the war is over, France will help Israel build a nuclear reactor.

Later, Israel will acquire a large fleet of French Mystere Jets, but that's another story.

Naturally, Egypt and Israel will each claim she won the war.

But History is a tale told by the winners. But sometimes it is a bitter regret related by those who lose.

And the losers always want revenge.

And tales of vengeance endure long after the retribution is redressed.

During the long history of recorded time, there are winners, losers, and those who still have hope. Each maintains a faith which its mythologies, cultures, and religions preserve. Thus, victories and defeats are rounded by dreams and sustain the winners, the defeated, and the forever unfulfilled.

And years later, I will learn that it was Ishmael's delivery of the intelligence file containing the plans of Operation Hand of Samson that affected Egypt's Sinai campaign, Israel's future, David's sacrifice, Rebecca's despair, her son's inheritance, and Hannah's and my dreams.

Simon

KADDISH

NOVEMBER 1956

When wars end, memorial services begin. *Dulce et decorum est pro patria mori* is the lie Horace trumpeted and Wilfred Owen exposed. Why do humans think it is honorable to die for one's country? Do we honor the memory of those who have died in battle because we are grateful that we can go on living on land they died to defend? Is it to comfort us, the living, who must live with our losses? To the victor belongs the triumphant grief. If everyone dies to defend his or her country, who is left? I survived this conflict, but how many have to die so the rest of us can exist? How can I live with this burden? How can any of us? So to assuage our anguish we give posthumous medals and glowing tributes to commemorate the sacrifices of the dead: we grateful, we sad few, we band of mourners.

Before the service begins I ask the commander of my paratroop unit if I can recite the eulogy to commemorate David's heroic action at the Mitla Pass. He is about to refuse when I fix him with such a fierce gaze that he dare not say no. Without a word, my expression silently conveys to him that I am the only person who knows that David did not volunteer to drive into the Egyptian forces as his propaganda squad proclaims, but undertook the suicide mission on his explicit order. My commander has no choice but to add my speech to the agenda.

I cynically listen to all the diplomats express their clichéd platitudes which praise the strong, brave, unselfish dead, and detail what their heroic deeds accomplished as the living, who never take part in battle, always do. When it is my turn to approach the podium, I see my friend's sacrificial flaming body exploding before my eyes. I pause for a moment to gaze solemnly at Rebecca, her parents, her younger brother, and her aunt and uncle who are sitting beside Prime Minister Ben Gurion and Defense Minister Dayan in the front row. I glare malevolently at Sharon who stares defiantly back at me. I continue to look at all of them as I say:

> My Friend David Silverman
> He was the dreamer, Israel his dream
> The Lion of Judah, the Phoenix in flames,
> The Hand of Samson, forged by a vision,
> Strength arose where weakness had never been
> His wish a power, his thought a deed.
> He bore the weight of history, the struggle of his people,
> He will rise from the ashes and become
> An eternal beacon, luminous throughout the ages.

Slowly I descend from the stage and sit down beside Rebecca. I scarcely hear the rest of the service. The words generals proclaim at memorial services are always the same; only the names and nationalities are different.

At the end of the interminable speeches we all file into the reception room for coffee and cake. Hannah always used to say, "My definition of a Jew is someone who feeds you before you sit down to eat." Now we Jews honor the dead with words they can't hear, medals they can't wear, and food they can't eat.

I find Rebecca sitting disconsolately in a corner. She has erected an invisible barrier around herself which all the mourners in the room except me knows they dare not break through. I sit beside her for a long while and then finally whisper apologetically, "I could write a poem about David, but I simply cannot write anything about Hannah.

"Losing her will haunt me forever. I didn't know how much I loved her until she was gone. Sometimes I see a phantom, and I think it is her dancing on the beach, cracking jokes, being adorably impudent; then I realize I am only looking at a shadow that walks along a wall..."

Rebecca puts her hand on mine and looks at my grief-stricken face. The tears are streaming down her cheeks. "I know. It's too soon. My parents are absolutely lost. To lose one child is horrible. To lose two in the same war is too much for anyone to bear. I am afraid to mourn for my brother and sister in front of them, because then we will all go mad."

"I asked Hannah to marry me the night before we mobilized. We were planning to tell everyone after the war was over."

"Simon, she told me, but swore me to secrecy. Don't be upset that she didn't keep your secret, but she was so happy she just had to tell someone. Anyhow, we all knew you two were meant for each other."

I gently take her hand in mine and we both sit silently in the middle of the commemorative crush of living mourners who know they owe their lives and homes to the dead. Then, as everyone begins to file out of the hall Rebecca startles me when she asks, "Simon, have you any idea where Isaac went for basic training?"

"Somewhere near the West Bank, south of Tel Aviv. Why?"

I haven't heard from Isaac since he left Ashkelon. I was hoping he would come to the memorial service."

"I don't know if he can get leave from basic training. Maybe he hasn't heard that David and Hannah died. Boot camp is incredibly strenuous; I had no break for the first three months."

"Three months! I can't wait that long."

I glance at her in astonishment. "Your brother and sister just died and all you can think about is Isaac, a boy you scarcely know."

"Simon, you don't understand." Her eyes bored into mine. "I can't wait three months. I might be showing by then."

I whistle in amazement. "I had no idea. You and he were that close?"

"I also thought the night before he left that we would get married when the war was over. And I haven't heard from him since then. Of course, he doesn't even know I'm pregnant."

Her anxiety and desperation are so acute that for the first time that week I look at another grieving person and do not think of my own loss. All week I had hated the nurses and soldiers who had survived the war and were celebrating the victory. All week I despised the paratroopers in my unit who were praising David's bravery and act of self-sacrifice.

How can a dog, a horse, a rat be alive if they are dead? Ever since Hannah died I have thought seriously about dying myself. Why live if Hannah is gone? How can I live with the knowledge that my best friend sacrificed himself to save my life?

I want to slap anyone who laughs or smiles or tells a joke. Now, with agonizing insight I realize that other people's suffering is as great as my own. I curse myself for my insensitivity and put my arm around her shoulder.

"I'll find him. Don't worry. If I can't, your uncle will know how to track Isaac. He could be on a two-week training exercise somewhere in the desert."

"Don't involve my uncle. I don't want anyone to know I'm going to have a baby. If my parents or aunt and uncle find out, they'll be devastated. The grief they feel over losing David and Hannah is a proud grief. They died heroic deaths. My pregnancy will bring nothing but shame to the family."

"After the mourning period is over, I'll find out how to get in touch with Isaac. He wouldn't desert you. The news of David's and Hannah's deaths hasn't reached him. He's just too busy to contact you. Basic training is stressful and demanding. And wherever he is, I know he's thinking about you. He was with you day and night before he left. Come on, your parents are waiting."

Gently, I put my arm around her shoulder and together we walk over to her family. But I can't help but think, *That bastard, he seduced her, and then he left her.*

Just before we reach the vestibule where her parents and uncle are standing I see General Dayan go over to Rebecca's father to offer his condolences.

As we approach her parents she barely acknowledges Dayan's expression of sympathy and automatically shakes hands with Prime Minister Ben Gurion. Dimly she becomes aware that he is talking to her about her golden Star of David necklace that is gleaming in the sunlight against her black blouse.

"Yes," she tells Ben Gurion and Dayan, "it is an unusual necklace. Someday I'll tell you why the cross is attached to its back."

Rebecca

SUSPICION?

NOVEMBER 1956

As Dayan is commenting about my necklace an embryonic idea begins to germinate in my tortured mind. I remembered that Isaac had said that if I had a Muslim husband I could then weld a Muslim crescent unto the necklace to make it truly representative of the people who lived in Palestine.

"Palestine!" He said Palestine, not Israel. I was so hurt that he thought I could marry a Muslim that I didn't ask him at that moment why he called our country Palestine. Later when I did question him he said with a strange expression that a Muslim would not call the land Israel and he was just trying to be authentic. I had thought his expression and behavior odd at the time, but I accepted his answer as understandably tolerant, if decidedly unpatriotic.

Suddenly, I realize that he never told me anything about his family or his background except that they were teachers in England. But he had eagerly talked to David and Simon at every opportunity about the possible mobilization dates and possible routes the army could take to invade Jordan or Egypt. He had avidly discussed the pros and cons of Russian, French and American jets with my uncle, who was amazed at Isaac's knowledge of the varying strengths and weaknesses of each type of aircraft.

How amused I had been that he didn't know the Israeli dances and folk songs that day at the beach.

Grasping the necklace in my hand I sit down weakly in the nearest chair. Tortured thoughts pulse through my throbbing brain.

David and Simon

FROM RUSSIA WITH LOVE

NOVEMBER 1956

Every five-year-old boy thinks it is his sacred duty to exasperate his family. He is genetically programmed to cause so much havoc that his bewildered parents wonder what they did to deserve this imp in their midst. One five-year-old creates tumultuous disruptions with glee, but two can creatively construct calamities on a scale that makes parents long for the calm of volcanic catastrophes.

When Stalin gave the Silverman family permission to leave the little village of Talmenka in the Altai Mountains of Southwestern Siberia and return to their native Poland after World War II, David was just such an impish five-year-old. Bored by the interminably long train ride through the bleak, desolate landscape he and his family were relieved to reach Novosibirsk, the largest urban center in this vast region of northern Asia east of the Russian Ural Mountains.

The little boy tortured his parents with his constant "Are we there, yet?" which is the mantra for every pest. He gave his mother a humiliating headache when he beat her in three successive games of chess. Now it is one thing to be beaten constantly by a friend or a husband, but when one's precocious preschooler is the source of such embarrassing humiliation the only refuge is to plead a migraine and retreat to a hidden corner with a chess manual. Naturally, David's mother had no such manual and she wondered, with desperation and a great deal of pride, how she was going to survive the rest of the trip.

This kid is going to drive me crazy, she thought. *What I wouldn't give for just a few peaceful minutes with a boring, unimaginative child.*

His father and uncle were exhausted from the interminable stories, games, and songs they had to tell him to keep him amused. Finally, the entire family was grateful when David found another five-year-old boy in the same railroad car and formed a fast friendship with him.

Simon Neuwirth's family, like David's, were Jewish-Polish refugees who had escaped from the Nazis by fleeing to Russia. The two little boys, coming from families with similar backgrounds, were well equipped with mischievous genes. When the train pulled into Novosibirsk's huge train terminal, both sets of parents told their sons, "Stay right here in your seats while we go to buy some fresh food."

It is against the code of the five-year-old boy to do as he is told, and these boys always honored the code. As soon as their parents were out of sight David and Simon, giggling conspirators, left the train to explore the vast terminal.

While a large passenger train blocked their view of the left side of the platform, they could see that the right side had four sets of tracks filled with awe-inspiring locomotives consisting of hundreds of cars. Wonderingly, they gazed upon the crowds of people who were thronging up the staircases leading from the loading platforms to the busy streets of a city which was larger than anything they had ever believed could have existed. Never had they seen such a building as the gleaming block-long white train station with its gigantic arched-windowed door that seemed hundreds of feet high.

Simon whispers in awe, "My father told me stories about a group of people called Cossacks who live near our village. They are huge warriors with large black mustaches who ride magnificent white stallions and protect the Czar.

"Only these giant Cossacks," Simon says, "could build this big, big building."

"Why would men who ride horses build a train terminal?" asks David.

Involved in their discussion about the identity of the possible builders of the terminal and fascinated by the crowds, noise, and blaring engine whistles they wandered further and further from their own railroad car.

Suddenly, David saw a boy of about 14 running from the top of one railroad freight car to another. Simon pointed excitedly to a policeman, crippled by too much vodka and sausage, several cars behind the boy. The obese lawman shouted repeatedly to the fugitive teen to stop, but the boy leaped nimbly from car to car. David and Simon held their breath each time the obese officer jumped from one train to another; they were certain the child would escape, and the officer would collapse in breathless defeat.

When the boy reached the last railroad car his only choices were either to allow himself to be apprehended by the determined policeman whose mustache bristled fiercely across the entire width of his broad, frost-reddened cheeks or jump what seemed to the boys like an immeasurable distance from the top of the car to the ground and continue to run away.

Tensely, David and Simon waited to see what would happen.

"What could the boy have done," David asked Simon, "to be chased by this Russian giant? Is he Jewish?"

The children immediately sympathized with him and prayed he would escape. Just when it appeared that the boy would allow himself to be caught, he jumped the 12 or so feet from the roof of the car onto the railroad tracks in front of the train. As soon as he landed in a heap on the tracks, the train began to move, and the wheels made a horrifying sound as they ground over his legs.

Years later, when David saw his first plate of spaghetti and tomato sauce, he was reminded of the image he had of the boy's legs when the suddenly penitent, horror-stricken policeman and several porters quickly pulled the screaming child off the tracks before the next set of wheels of the slowly moving train could do any further damage.

The boys waited and watched until a speeding ambulance arrived. The medical attendants who sprang like charging horses from its back door hastily put the hemorrhaging boy on a stretcher and shoved him into its rear compartment. Never before had David and Simon heard the ominous two-note siren blare its warning to all traffic to clear the roads. Too frightened to move, they stood by the tracks long after the ambulance had sped away. Not only did the scene they had just witnessed horrify them, but they also realized they were hopelessly lost and had no idea how to return to their own railroad car.

Suddenly, each felt an angry hand grab his shoulder. "Where the hell have you been?" David's father shouted at them. "We've been searching for you everywhere in this damn place for the last half hour." Grabbing each boy by the wrist, he harshly pulled both of them along the platform toward their train around which an enraged crowd had gathered. The boys saw the same policeman who had been chasing the boy was now shouting, "Where is that damn Jew?"

David quickly learned that the "damn Jew" was none other than his deaf uncle, Moishe, who had cleverly disabled the train's brake cable to prevent it from leaving the station. When the Silvermans and Neuwirths discovered that David and Simon were missing they had vainly pleaded with the engineer to delay the train's departure to give them time to find their missing boys.

"Why can't you Jews watch your lousy children? I can't hold up a train with hundreds of passengers because of two boys. I have a schedule to keep," the engineer had shouted without the slightest trace of sympathy. When Moishe realized the train would leave without them, he sabotaged the train's brakes. As the repairmen tried to fix them, David's father desperately searched the immense train station for the children.

With the train's departure now delayed until the necessary repair could be made, much to the annoyance of unsympathetic passengers and outraged train personnel, David's father had the luxury of an extra half-hour to search for him and Simon.

But a porter had seen Moishe tamper with the brakes and reported to the police that the deaf man had deliberately broken the cable. Shouting that the Silverman family was responsible for the train's delay, the crowd was in a vengeful mood, and Sarah became extremely frightened. She was afraid that the volatile Jewish refugees, anxious to leave Russia and return to their pre-war homes, would do to them what Hitler had not. She also was frantically worried about the whereabouts of her son and his friend.

She and Naomi Neuwirth begged the crowd to be patient, and when the tearful mothers explained to the disgruntled passengers why Moishe had tampered with the brakes they gained some sympathy from those who also were parents. To her immense relief, her angry husband appeared with the two tearful boys in tow just when the repairman declared that the cable was now in good working order. The passengers climbed aboard, and once the train was underway again, no one was interested any longer in punishing the saboteur.

Hearing a few people chuckling to themselves about how clever Moishe was gave Aaron and Sarah some peace of mind. An hour later, reassured that the police, conductor, and passengers seemed to have given up all thoughts of arresting, or even, as some had threatened, lynching him now that the train was speeding down the track, Moishe appeared from a hiding-place whose whereabouts David never learned, despite repeated questioning.

The two boys were given a severe tongue-lashing by their relieved families and warned to behave for the rest of the trip – a warning that no adult believed would be heeded and, of course, that neither child intended to obey. But the incident cemented the already fast growing friendship and the two boys became inseparable. Simon's mother often joked that Siamese twins were not as close to each other as David was to her son. David's mother lamented that Satan himself would be horrified by the deviltry the two boys could concoct. And both mothers were thrilled that their sons were so close. Finally, they stopped exasperating their families with their precocious, mischievous behavior, and started concocting ingenious and imaginative games which amused the sometimes, but not always, tolerant adults.

When the two families arrived in Poland, they found that the Communists had confiscated all their possessions. Devastated by the anti-Semitism in their town that seemed even worse now than it had been before the war, the Silvermans and Neuwirths decided to immigrate together to Israel.

David's family was placed in temporary barracks on the outskirts of Ashkelon until Aaron could find a job and buy a home while the Neuwirths went to live in an Ulpan near Tel Aviv. Set up by the State of Israel in many areas of the country, the Ulpan is a unique institution whose purpose is to immerse immigrants in the Hebrew language and help them to assimilate into Israeli culture. Thus, Simon and David were separated for about a year while their fathers learned enough Hebrew to enable them to find jobs, purchase houses, and feel less like strangers in their new homeland.

When the two families found homes near each other in Ashkelon, Hannah and Rebecca had already joined the Silverman family. The Neuwirths were told that kind Christians had hidden Rebecca from the Germans, which actually was the truth. Since no one in Ashkelon had known Sarah before she arrived in Israel, she told everyone that Hannah was her baby. Naomi and Jacob Neuwirth were upset that she had not told them she was pregnant, but she told them that the pregnancy had been a very difficult one, and she was afraid she would miscarry. Therefore, she had not told anyone she was expecting a child.

"Then," she lied, "Hannah was born three months early, and the doctors were not sure that she would live." She told them that Hannah had had to stay in the hospital many weeks until she gained several pounds and the doctor thought she was mature enough to live outside an incubator. The Neuwirths accepted this explanation, but Naomi thought she had never seen a fatter, healthier baby who did not look like either of her parents.

Since Hannah was David's younger sister, Simon had hundreds of opportunities to tease her mercilessly. She never let him forget that once, when he and David were seven, they were talking about the train incident, and she had innocently inquired why they were so upset about it, Simon had haughtily told her, "Oh, that happened before you were born. You're too young to know about anything so important." The four-year-old girl's feelings were crushed, and she carried a grudge against him for years.

This amused Simon. For many years she was nothing more than the bratty, pesky kid sister of his best friend. And then, without his realizing it, she blossomed into a green-eyed, reddish-blonde, beautiful young girl with a captivating smile. He didn't notice when his teasing stopped and his courting began. One day, with a broad smile, David's mother asked him whom he came now to their house to see: David or Hannah? Suddenly, he realized that his feelings for Hannah went beyond friendship. The Silvermans heartily approved of his relationship with Hannah just as they had welcomed his friendship with David. Sarah Silverman and Naomi Neuwirth, already very good friends, relished the thought of being *machatanisters*, a Jewish term denoting the relationship between the parents of children who are married to each other.

Therefore, the dreaded knock on the door by representatives of the Israeli government reverberated through both the Silverman and Neuwirth houses. When the earnest young official and the sympathetic nurse, whose job it was to notify all the relatives of those killed in the fighting, told Sarah and Aaron that their son, David, and daughter, Hannah, had died in the Suez War, the inconsolable parents knew that Simon, also, would be devastated. They had lost a son and a daughter, and the young man had lost his best friend and his fiancée.

Together the grieving mourners somehow endured the memorial service and the two sets of parents drew even closer. The Silvermans withdrew from all their social and business activities and could only share their immense grief with the Neuwirths. Yet, they were astounded when Rebecca and Simon announced their engagement. Sarah Silverman, at first, saw the betrothal as a betrayal of Hannah's memory. She wondered if Rebecca and Simon really loved each other. She had been well aware of her daughter's feelings for Isaac and was concerned that the marriage was founded on grief and loss, instead of love and respect. Although Rebecca was chronologically two years older than Simon, temperamentally, she was less mature. Despite all advice to the contrary, the two were adamant in their determination to marry. Reluctantly, the parents consented, and a brief, sad wedding took place a month after Hannah's funeral.

Sarah was quite surprised when she learned Rebecca was pregnant so soon after the marriage, but her daughter told her that because Simon was often patrolling in a dangerous area on the Israeli-Syrian border they had decided to have a child as quickly as possible.

"With death all around us, I want to have someone to remember my baby's father by in case anything happens to Simon," she told her mother.

"Oh, I see," said Sarah. She did not dare ask her daughter the one question uppermost in her suspicious mind. *Is Simon the father the child will remind you of?*

Simon
DREAM DEFERRED
NOVEMBER 1956

A ll my life I adored three people: Hannah Silverman, the little sister of my best friend, David; Hannah Silverman, the sabra; and Hannah Silverman, the actress and dancer.

Since David was my best friend and everyone related to David was dear to me, I always regarded Hannah as special. I had been amazed when I noted that despite the great age difference between the elder Silverman children and Hannah there was no sibling rivalry or jealousy between them and their little sister. Since they spoiled and loved her as much as the adults did, I felt Hannah deserved my undying love and loyalty just because she was my best friend's little sister. My attachment to David went beyond mere friendship. The incident in the Novosibirsk railway station and the experiences we had on the long train ride from Siberia to Poland had forged a bond between us that no one else could share. Also, as the only child of two very quiet parents who were not emotionally demonstrative, I loved the hubbub and commotion always present in the Silverman household.

And who caused most of the commotion? Hannah, of course! Whenever mischief was brewing, Hannah was the instigator. Whenever gloom threatened to darken everyone's mood, Hannah's infectious smile and bubbling personality gave everyone an emotional lift. To hide my fondness for her, I constantly called her "Green Eyes" and teased her mercilessly about her freckles. I never let her know that I thought her reddish-blonde hair was a beacon that glowed in a house filled with dark-haired, brown-eyed, olive-skinned people. When she was little she reminded me of a golden imp. As she grew older and slowly transformed from a tomboy into a lovely young girl, her blonde hair and golden skin enchanted me and I found myself becoming mesmerized by her beauty.

I always felt the sabras in Israel were a special breed. They were the young, strong natives who took their name from the prickly pears that grow on the sabra cactus which dot the desert landscape. Thorns on the skin of this plant protect the sweet fruit lying just under its thick peel. The early Israeli pioneers saw the sabra pear as a metaphor for the kind of person needed to tame the raw, undeveloped country and make it bloom.

Always conscious that I had not been born in Israel, I envied the confident, brash, thorny natives who overcame every obstacle both nature and politicians put in their way. Nothing intimidated them, nothing overawed them, nothing defeated them. They were going to forge a nation from a pile of stones, mounds of sand, a dead sea, and forty million hostile Arabs weren't going to stop them. Yet underneath their cocky assuredness and brazen attitudes were sweet, loving natures, and if anyone was the epitome of the typical sabra, it was Hannah.

I adored her caustic wit and sarcastic brand of humor. Although she was determined to get her own way, she always did it with such diplomacy and humor that no one was ever annoyed. I could only laugh and acquiesce to her every whim when she informed me that she was forceful, determined, and strong-willed, while everyone else was stubborn, headstrong and obstinate.

Semantics was always her strong point.

As she developed into a lithesome, sensual teenager with a dancer's quick grace, I was astounded by the feelings she aroused in me. No longer did she merely amuse me as the kid sister of my best friend. Now I saw her as a woman to be idolized, an actress who could command the attention of an entire audience with her charismatic stage presence. And to my amazement she returned my adoration.

Our relationship changed from light-hearted bantering and gentle teasing during the summer we were in rehearsals for *Showboat*. Hannah had the role of Parthy Hawks, and I was Captain Andy, her husband. She loved playing the part of the headstrong, feisty wife of the riverboat captain as much as I loved playing her doting but henpecked husband. After rehearsal every night I walked her home, and these nights were the first time we were not constantly surrounded by the other members of her family. Although Rebecca was also in the play, her scenes were seldom run through at the same time as ours, so we were able to enjoy a privacy and intimacy we had never experienced before.

After the play completed its run, I was inducted into the army, and Hannah returned to high school to finish her senior year. The following summer our relationship deepened, and I sensed that all the Silvermans were pleased that Hannah and I spent so much time together. Whenever I was on leave from my unit and visited them, ostensibly to give them news about David, who was also in my paratroop squad, Rebecca would find a reason to leave Hannah and me alone.

Could anyone have a better sister?

The night before we mobilized for the attack in the Sinai Peninsula I asked Hannah to marry me. I knew her medical unit was also activated; both of us were apprehensive, yet filled with the defiant courage that can only belong to the very young who have never experienced defeat and know we never will.

We excitedly planned our wedding, which we would hold after the war was over, and she finished her tour of duty. I knew Hannah, bursting with happiness, would run home to tell Rebecca that I had asked her to marry me, and later that night she called to tell me Rebecca was in love with Isaac. The girls romantically dreamed of having a double wedding.

"Now, if only David can find a girl," she giggled, "everything will be perfect."

We planned to invite all our relatives to the café for drinks on the first Sabbath afternoon after the war was over. In the presence of both our families I would give Hannah the beautiful antique diamond engagement ring which belonged to my grandmother. Every time my mother sees this ring on Hannah's finger she'll remember her beloved mother and know it is worn by the woman her son loves. The ring will symbolize the love that flows from generation to generation.

I could see Hannah's father and uncle congratulating me. The women would all glow with pride. Who else but David would be my best man?

As soon as I asked Hannah to marry me, she was already planning what dresses Rebecca and she would wear. Woman, thy name is vanity.

When I saw David die, and then learned that Hannah was killed when a jeep in which she was riding had run over a land mine, I became almost insane with grief. I blamed myself for David's death. I was sure that the only reason David sacrificed his life was to enable me to escape from the Mitla Pass and return to Ashkelon and marry Hannah. Over and over I thought, *if I hadn't told him that I asked Hannah to be my wife, he wouldn't have driven the jeep into the Egyptian line. He wouldn't have sacrificed his life to save mine. How he must have loved Hannah.*

Immediately after the memorial service for David, Rebecca and I walk to the cemetery for Hannah's burial service.

We can't bury David. The Mitla Pass cremated him, and his ashes will blend into the desert together with the Egyptian soldiers he incinerated. He is now an inextricable part of the sand that pulverizes and blasts the rocks of the Sinai where our ancestors wandered for 40 years. His life ended in fire, and I feel as if mine will end in ice.

The road to Hannah's graveyard is lined on both sides with fragrant orange trees in full bloom. The air is filled with the scent of the white blossoms and the buzzing of honeybees. But Rebecca and I are numb to the beauty that surrounds us. All we blindly see are the many graves topped by marble trees with their top branches cut off in lieu of regular tombstones. Each marble tree is missing its full complement of branches to symbolize that the young person buried in the grave died before he or she lived a full complement of years. In fact, most of the dead who have a marble tree for a tombstone never reached their twentieth year. Almost all of them were soldiers who either died in the War for Independence in 1948 or in terrorist attacks.

Rebecca and I follow the throng of people to Hannah's grave and stand silently while the rabbi intones the platitudes one typically says at a funeral service. Then each of the family members and I shovel a clod of dirt into the grave.

Rebecca whispers to me, "If the baby is a girl I'm going to name her Hannah."

"If it's a boy will you name it David?" I ask.

"I don't know. If I find out that Isaac is dead, I would like to name him after Isaac. But what if I learn he's alive, but, for some reason he never comes back to me? And if he is alive and has deserted me, how can I give an illegitimate child my sister's or my brother's name? How can I have an illegitimate child? My parents will be so ashamed of me. My aunt and uncle will be disgraced. Simon, Simon, what can I do?"

I look at her and my heart melts. She looks so desperate, so woebegone, so grief-stricken that I realize her agony is greater than my own.

"Rebecca," I whisper, "don't worry. If Isaac doesn't come back, I will take care of you. I will not let David, Hannah, or you ever be dishonored. Give me a week to try to find him. If I can't locate him in that time, or I find out that he is dead we'll announce our engagement."

"It won't work. Everyone knows you loved Hannah. They'll be suspicious if we get married and then I start to show right after the wedding. Anyhow, we can't get married before a year of mourning is over."

"Wrong. We can get married, but we can't have any music or dancing at the wedding. And you know how much I love to dance," I say with the first smile I am able to produce since Hannah died. "We'll tell everyone that since married women don't serve in the army I thought it was a good way to make sure you are out of harm's way. Your parents should welcome that idea. When you begin to show, we'll say we wanted to have a baby right away to perpetuate Hannah's or David's memory."

"There's one more thing, Simon. We like each other, but we're not in love. We'll have Isaac's and Hannah's ghosts haunting us. What will that do to our marriage? How will that make you treat this baby? At best you may resent it. At worst you might hate it. You may grow to dislike me because I'm not Hannah, and you will feel trapped."

"I was thinking about this for the last half hour as we were walking to Hannah's grave. Isaac isn't going to come back. He must be dead, and neither his parents nor anyone in the army realizes that you should be notified. And you need an immediate solution."

"Let's be moral and honest about our situation," I say bluntly. "I do not feel trapped. Nothing or no one is preventing me from going away and never seeing you again. I asked you to marry me because I want to help you, not only to save you and your family from disgrace, but because I realize I do care for you. Not the way I cared for Hannah; I don't think I'll ever love anyone the way I loved her, but that doesn't mean I can't have feelings for you.

"But you must know this or our marriage will be based on false premises. I feel responsible for David's death. If I hadn't told him I was going to marry Hannah, I don't think he would have sacrificed himself so I could escape the hell that was the Mitla Pass. He died to enable me to live and care for her. I owe him a life, and I am marrying you partly to repay my debt to him by saving his family's name from disgrace. Can you accept that?"

"And," I continue before she can answer me, "I will not resent the child. While he is partly Isaac's he is also half yours and by extension, also a part of David and Hannah. Naturally, I know I can't love this baby as I will a child who is mine, but he or she will never know that. I promise you on Hannah's grave that I will give the child a good home and be a proper parent to him or her."

Rebecca gives me a look filled with grief, resignation, and relief. "I don't want you to blame yourself for David's impulsive act. If he died to save the unit, that was his choice. He loved the Lions and the paratroopers. And he was an officer. I know David; I'm sure he felt he had to safeguard all his men, not just his sister's fiancé. And Simon," she said earnestly, "I will be a good wife to you. I do care for you. I will never cause you any shame or embarrassment."

I look at her and think *what a forlorn pair we are.* But I realize that this marriage may save my sanity.

Without the need to protect Rebecca and her child, I don't know how I will survive.

Together the two of us, filled with a dark sensibility of our past and future, stand at the edge of Hannah's grave. Both of us are aware that each is providing salvation for the other. While our grief over the loss of David, Hannah, and Isaac will never diminish, I hope our marriage born from turbulent need, will heal us. Death has divided us from those we love, and we, the living, must survive despite the bitter loss of that love, despite the bitter betrayals life gives us, despite the incomprehensible fate existence has in store for each of us.

Ishmael

FAIR IS FOUL, AND FOUL IS FAIR

LONDON, NOVEMBER 1956

I look around my flat on Brompton Road in the comfortable middle-class section of Kensington, located not too far from the center of the City of London and think the constant damp English drizzle is just as intolerable as the unrelenting Israeli sun.

Although this isn't a luxury hotel on the Riviera that James Bond would stay in, I'm definitely making progress. The furnishings, while not luxurious, are upscale. But Egyptian Intelligence in Britain is not as sophisticated as our division in Israel. It took me a full minute to find the bugs Omar planted in my room in Ashkelon. I found the microphone some inept member of our unit here secreted in the lamp base on the night table in only five seconds.

A ten-year-old could detect the device placed in the telephone earpiece. I must remember to call bored diplomats' wives and ask them provocatively sexy questions or invite one up for tea. Intelligence, after all, should get voyeuristic thrills while they listen to my conversations with jaded women.

Lining the street are classic white townhouses guarded by black wrought iron gates. My apartment is near an Arab candy shop whose shelves are filled with huge round wheels of halvah stuffed with pistachios and dried maraschino cherries. What fascinates me most in the window of the shop is an ingenious windmill made entirely of chocolate. The uppermost sail is in the shape of a little Dutch boy and the bottom sail sports a delightful little Dutch girl with flying lemon yellow pigtails as she revolves on her dark brown tower. The windmill is set in a rose garden in which the flowers are made entirely of chocolate dyed red whose stems sprout mint green leaves. Over the doorway the shop proudly bears the sign, "Purveyors to Her Majesty, Queen Elizabeth II."

The Queen, I think, *has good taste, even if she is always surrounded by those stupid corgis. What is this Western fascination with dogs?*

My flat is only three blocks from the underground where I board a train every weekday to travel to the London School of Economics on Houghton Street. There, I either attend a lecture or go to the library to find material for my research paper on the geographic, economic, and sociological impact the Nile River has on modern Egypt.

Every Saturday evening I meet with a few other Egyptians to go, as the English quaintly say, pub crawling. No one thinks my weekly meetings with my tutor are out of the ordinary since all students see their tutors periodically to review their progress on the mandatory thesis, which forms the largest part of the grade for the course.

My tutor is Edward Henry, an old friend from Borough High Street in Southwark, the British Secret Intelligence School for training spies. Henry is a double agent; what the British call a rounder or a mole. Born in the wealthy London suburb of Mayfair to an aristocratic British mother and an Egyptian diplomat named Ahmed Hassim, Henry regally Anglicized his last name, attended Cambridge University, and came to admire the ideals of Lenin and Stalin. At Cambridge he met Anthony Blunt, Guy Burgess, Donald Maclean, and Kim Philby. All of them served for years in British Secret Intelligence, but actually were double agents for Russia, and Henry was instrumental in recruiting them to work for MI6 in order to betray England.

In 1949 Henry's good friend Ken Peters became the first secretary of the British Embassy in Washington with access to the highest Anglo-American security matters. During the next few years Peters passed sensitive documents detailing information vital to Egyptian security to Henry, who passed them on to couriers like me in the Egyptian Secret Service.

Both Henry and I are angered at England's audacity and egotistic attitude towards every other culture. Britannia thinks that she and only she is the arbiter of civilization, politics, religion, and fashion. She scorns the traditions of the myriad Native American and African tribes, the Indian, the Irish, the Welsh, the Australian aborigines, the Maoris, the … I cannot even enumerate them all.

The English think the sun never sets on their Empire. We Egyptians want to make sure it never rises again. While I relish destroying the British superior attitude and their colonial mindset, Henry has an even more personal reason to upset MI6's plans in the Middle East.

The first time Henry and I met, he insisted on telling me how much he hated going to his mother's ancestral home in Mayfair for dinner. "It was even worse when we went to their country estate in Kent. Every time my father and I went to my mother's parents' manor we were made to feel as though we were second-class citizens who could never match the nobility of their centuries old British aristocracy.

"I remember how intimidating my maternal grandmother was. She sat me down on her endless Anglo-Saxon lap after dinner and read this poem to me:

Foreign Children
Little Indian, Sioux, or Crow
Little frosty Eskimo
Little Turk or Japanee,
Oh! don't you wish that you were me?
You have seen the scarlet trees
And the lions overseas;
You have eaten ostrich eggs,'
And turned the turtles off their legs.
Such a life is very fine,
But it's not so nice as mine:
You must often as you trod,
Have wearied NOT to be abroad.
You have curious things to eat,
I am fed on proper meat;

You must dwell upon the foam,
But I am safe and live at home.
Little Indian, Sioux or Crow,
Little frosty Eskimo,
Little Turk or Japanee
Oh! Don't you wish that you were me?"

"You still remember that poem?" I ask.

"I never forgot it or the humiliation I suffered. She made a point of calling me 'Ahmed, the Egyptian child,' and made it obvious that I am not, nor ever will be completely British no matter how much I try to assimilate. Whenever my cousins, Colin, Nigel, Charles, and Pamela recited that poem, and grandmother made all of us memorize it, I always felt that they were saying directly to me 'Oh! Don't you wish that you were me?'

I detest their goddam British aristocratic superiority. I hate the way they treated my father. I loathe the way they looked down on my mother for marrying 'beneath her' as my grandfather put it so succinctly. I abhor the way my blue-eyed cousins referred to me as the 'dark one.' Most of all, I am disgusted by the way the British think they can come into Africa and civilize it. I can't stand the Jews, but I admire the way one of them, Disraeli, put those anti-Semitic aristocrats in their place."

"How did he do that?" I know, but Henry is someone who must feel superior to me. I am fully aware his ego needs that.

"He stood up in Parliament and told them that his ancestors were lawyers, doctors, and philosophers when the British were pagans running around in the woods sporting blue tattoos and wearing animal skins. I'll tell you one thing about the Jews – they don't let the British push them around. And we're not going to let them dominate us in Egypt anymore."

Every week Henry meets with me and every week I send my report to Egyptian intelligence.

Loneliness, not espionage, however, is uppermost in my mind. My mornings, afternoons and evenings are filled with visions of Rebecca.

I dream about her every night and imagine she is lying beside me in my bed. Each morning I fantasize that she is eating breakfast with me at my little table in this tiny kitchen and every afternoon picture her walking beside me as I stroll the byways of a city built for pedestrians. Every woman I see cannot compare to her. I am desperately longing for the woman I know I am forbidden to love.

In the late fall I walk through the city streets filled with the dreary prophecy of November rain to avoid staying in my lonely apartment, and even though I appreciate the museums, the theatre, the gardens, and the architecture, I am homesick.

This rain-sodden, fog bound, cockneypolis makes me long for Cairo. She is the cradle of civilization, the home of the pyramids, the Sphinx, the Nile delta, and the oldest mall in the world: the Khan al Khalili, a street lined with myriad stalls and shops. Harrod's Department Store and Sloan Square cannot compete with the thousands of artifacts, both ancient and modern, that can be found in the bazaar's stalls. Vases bearing the image of the most beautiful woman of the ancient world, Queen Nefertiti, and the golden funeral mask of the young King Tut lie next to exquisitely tooled leather handbags, hand woven carpets and intricately wrought gold jewelry.

Tantalizing aromas from pungent spices and foods waft through the crowded, crooked streets. Rooflines project both ancient heaven-yearning minarets juxtaposed between modern sharply angled metal television antennas. Women wearing head scarves as well as those in high heels and western clothes throng the stalls looking for bargains. And the traffic! London at the height of rush hour will never equal Cairo's choked streets on a quiet afternoon.

The British lords excavated ancient Egyptian royal tombs and raped the pyramids. Weren't they surprised to learn how skilled my people were centuries before the savage Celts knew how to fashion rude log huts with thatched roofs and mud floors on their forlorn wuthering moors?

They filled their British Museum with art they stole from other civilizations. I plotted night after night to steal the Rosetta Stone and the gold statue of the donkey goddess Palés and bring both back to Cairo. Look at the beautiful marble statues that adorned the top gable of the Parthenon that Lord Elgin stole and placed here for all the tourists to gape at for a second and then move on. As a service to Cleopatra, our last Egyptian queen whose ancestors hailed from Greece, I dream of restoring them to their rightful place. It's the least I can do for a beautiful temptress.

I toured Westminster Abbey, the church built by Edward the Confessor in 1065 and was duly impressed, but how can it compare with the Mosque of Amr Ibn Al-As? The first Muslim house of prayer was built in Egypt in 642, according to my father. Thus, it predates Westminster by more than three centuries. This Abbey is nothing more than a monumental burial ground for mighty kings and queens. I chuckle when I see the statue of Queen Elizabeth I presiding regally in the north aisle of the Lady's Chapel while her adversarial cousin, Mary, Queen of Scots, holds court in the south aisle.

"What do you two queens say to each other now when the lights go down and the tourists leave? You two were prisoners of everlasting ambition; now you are captives of eternal death."

I paused respectfully in front of Sir Isaac Newton's, Charles Dickens' and Geoffrey Chaucer's markers and gave a passing glance to the prime ministers and royalty who are among the more than 3,000 people buried in the ancient edifice. But I am truly astounded to see that an actress, Dame Sybil Thorndike, is one of the people entombed in the Abbey. An actress! I can just see my father shaking his head in amazement over the decadence of the western infidels who would honor a woman of this lowly profession in such an exalted manner.

While Westminster is the church of the monarch of England, suitable for royal ceremonies, coronations, weddings and funerals it is also is the burial place of kings, statesmen, poets, scientists, soldiers, musicians and actors. But the Mosque would never be so defiled. My mosque is not only the Egyptian home of Islam, it is the first Moslem religious edifice built not only in Cairo, but in all Africa.

This most sacred building, where I worshipped many times with my father, contains magnificent gold mosaics, marble works, a silver-coated niche, and a moving pulpit. Nothing in London compares to it.

Look at the Thames River whose bridge is always falling down. It is a puny stream compared to the mighty Nile. What a magical waterway the source of Egypt's existence is! The paper I am compelled to write about the Nile to maintain my cover at the university is fascinating. I am researching the history of the ancient feluccas and modern steamboats, crocodiles and hippos, cataracts and dams that thrived throughout its course as the antediluvian river formed the lifeblood of my city, my people, my civilization. Her floodwaters make the soil rich and fertile and because of her, the desert blooms.

All through the bleak London winter I occupy myself by wandering through certain half-deserted streets and muttering retreats with insidious intent. But memories haunt me. Memories prevented me from betraying my homeland and made me betray Rebecca. Memories insure that no Paradise can compare to the place where I was born.

In my most depressed moment I think, *I penetrated Rebecca. I thrust into her. I made her bleed. She is the Israel I possessed once and will again.*

The truth is I miss loving her. And I love missing her.

Other times, I know I will never see her again, will never possess her once more. Rationality and irrationality between sons and lovers war with each other longer than any feuds between nations. England and France fought a war for just one hundred years. But the love-hate relationship between the descendants of Isaac and Ishmael will last forever.

By January I meet some Arabs who are friends of Henry at university. We spend long hours discussing political, religious, economic, or philosophical topics which keeps Rebecca's face from haunting me. I join the group, not only to laugh at their earnest inability to solve all the problems of the Middle East, but to acknowledge the fact that Marx was wrong: politics, not religion, is the opiate of the middle class.

In February, an intense young woman named Nuzhat Shakil who is in my economics class asks if she can join our group. Since she always asks questions that annoy our professor I agree. I notice that she saves all her caustic remarks for class, but is very quiet when she is with us. When she is not present, one of the group suggests that she might feel uncomfortable among so many men and encourages me to make an effort to include her in the conversation. So I sit next to her whenever she attends a meeting, and make a banal comment to which she always gives a passionate response that makes me look like an idiot.

During one of London's dreariest days I thank Allah that an extremely boring class is over. Even a biting comment of Nuzhat's doesn't disturb the equanimity of our pedantic Chinese professor, who can't seem to wrap his tongue around the word "utilitarianism." It took me 30 minutes to understand his pronunciation of that one word which he kept repeating over and over, and then I decided I wasn't interested in anything he or anyone else had to say.

As I leave the class in disgust, I notice with amusement that Nuzhat manages to bump into me. She pretends to be upset, so I invite her to have a cup of tea in a charming little shop across the street.

"Tell me all about Egypt," she asks as we sit by a window and gaze at the pouring rain which has begun to fall just as our tea and cakes arrive. "I can tell you're really homesick."

"Have you never been there?"

"No, my family came from India after the partition in 1948, along with many other Muslims. We did not want to go to Pakistan, and London University offered my father a position. Why did you come to England?"

"I am earning my master's degree in economics. How about you?"

"I am going to university to avoid a marriage my parents arranged for me. You may say I am studying political science."

"And how does attending university enable you to avoid your parents' plans?"

"I told them that as soon as I obtain my degree I will marry their fabulously rich friend whom they have picked out for me, and have the grandsons they yearn for. Somehow I always have to take another course, or I do so badly in my class that I receive no credit and must take it again."

"Doesn't your fiancé grow impatient?"

"No, as long as I am in school, he thinks he has complete freedom from a nagging wife, crying children, and meddling in-laws, and he can fulfill his 'needs,' as my mother calls them, every night as often as he wishes with any beautiful girl his money can buy."

"You are cynical."

"I have no illusions."

There is a strained silence between us. I try to break it with some trite conversation about the gloomy rain and the miserable English weather until Nuzhat finally asks, "Have your parents arranged a marriage for you?"

"Yes."

"Don't you hate the girl? Don't you resent your parents?"

"Actually, she's very beautiful, and we are deeply in love. In fact, I asked my father to arrange the match with her father."

"Lucky you. Are you sure she feels the same way about you?"

"Absolutely."

"Liar."

"Did you say you're majoring in political science? No wonder you have trouble passing your classes."

"I learned one fact: diplomats lie to protect the truth. Are you a diplomat?"

"If I tell the truth, you'll think I'm lying. If I lie, you'll think I'm lying. I'm the best diplomat you'll ever meet."

"I should marry you."

"And why is that?

"A woman should never marry a man she can trust."

"Why not? Shouldn't marriage be based on trust?"

"No, a husband I can trust is boring. Boredom kills relationships."

"You prefer excitement to faithfulness?"

"I'm not stupid. No one in this world is trustworthy. At least with you, I'd be sure you know how to lie to protect the truth."

"Betrayal doesn't bother you, Nuzhat? Then who can trust you?"

"No one can trust anyone," she says.

"Sorry, I can't live like that."

"Then you're either a saint or a fool."

"There's a difference, Nuzhat?"

"Yes, fools are stupid. Saints are stupider. They die for causes no one else believes in, a country that doesn't appreciate them, and a religion that kills them before they can be worshipped. At least fools are the wisest persons in plays, and traitors get some money and a few pages in a history book."

"Your husband will be lucky to have such a realist for a wife. You, however, will be the most unfortunate of all women."

"Why unfortunate? Since when is being a realist unlucky?"

"To love someone is to be lucky. Cynics can never love."

"If I can't love, my heart can't be broken."

"Hearts that can't be broken won't mind a little rain. Let's go."

"Then you won't marry me?

"And break your rich fiancé's heart?"

"I can't stand men who patronize me."

"See Nuzhat, already our relationship is in jeopardy."

"No, it's just getting interesting."

"Actually, you know why our parents arrange our marriages. It's to keep the class system intact. We marry their friends and this way the economic, social, religious, and political castes are stable. The rich stay rich, and when the poor rebel they only make circumstances worse for themselves. We are all prisoners of that powerful word: TRADITION."

"And you say I'm cynical."

"No, I study economics. I'm practical. You're the cynic."

"How about taking cynical me home?"

"No, but I'll walk you to the underground."

"You only want to walk with me because I have a brolly and you were too stupid to bring one."

"I keep thinking I'm still in Egypt, where it seldom rains."

She unfolds her huge, purple brolly; we huddle under it and walk towards the station. I feel so stupid walking under a purple umbrella with her.

Just as she is about to buy her ticket we hear a tremendous explosion and see crowds pouring out of the exit, followed by billows of acrid smelling smoke.

"What happened?" she shrieks to one of the escapees, as she grabs my hand.

The man, covered in black soot and blood, runs past us and yells, "The IRA placed a bomb on the tracks. It exploded when a train ran over it; hundreds are trapped inside the burning car. They're screaming and pounding on the doors and trying to break through the windows, but they'll never get out of that incinerator. Loads of people on the platform are injured, too. Get the hell out of here."

Joining the panic stricken crowd, we stampede down the street. I see a taxi driver at the street corner and jump into his cab's back seat pulling Nuzhat in with me.

I ask her for her address and give it to the driver. He glares at us and demands, "Are ye with the IRA?"

"Idiot," she screams. "Do we look Irish?"

"This is their doing, ye know," He glares malevolently back at the station, and then puts the car in gear. "Well, it's true. Ye dunna look Irish, that's for sure."

"How do you know the IRA planted the bomb?" Nuzhat asks.

"Who cares who planted the bomb? Let's go!" I yell. As we pull away from the curb an ambulance misses us by inches as it zooms toward the station. We all turn and watch it race up to the entrance. It screeches to a screaming stop; its back doors fling open, and masked gunmen jump out and start firing at the still-fleeing passengers. Our cab driver needs no further urging to gun his motor and race away.

The driver peers at us through his rearview mirror and asks in his broadest cockney accent, "Are ye Catholics? Know that I curse every Papist Irishman from Saint Patrick to James Joyce."

"We're not Catholics and have never been in Ireland," I say in my broadest Queen's Protestant English.

He looks at us and says, "You look like Jews. I hope you're not stingy tightwads with the tips. Them an' the Indians 'old on to their money. Now, your Arabs, they're big tippers."

"Why?" I ask, waiting to hear why I am expected to be generous. He knows damn well we're Muslims, and as far as he's concerned, all Muslims are Arabs.

"All that oil, ye know. They're floatin' on a sea of money."

At that moment we hear another explosion near Trafalgar Square. Our equal opportunity racist cabby forgets about his ethnic economic theories, which are more interesting than those of our college professor's utilitarian concepts, and guns his gas pedal.

He ignores every red light and accelerates at blinding speed through the yellow lights until we reach Nuzhat's flat. I give him a 25 percent tip, which he hastily accepts without a "thank you" and say, "Good luck, mate and stay away from the damned Irish Catholics. They either bore ye to death with their annoying stories about down-and-out Dubliners or blow ye up with their blasted bombs. We should have let them all starve in the potato famine."

He heads back to the underground station. Nothing like a tragedy to improve business. I wonder if he gives the same speech to all his customers, Gentiles or Jews, who might take umbrage at being called tightwads and give him a bigger tip than he deserves. Neat technique. Now that's utilitarianism.

I escort Nuzhat to her apartment and she invites me in. I don't want to spend any more time with her, but she still seems upset by the terrorist bombing, so I follow her into a dark, eerie, and sparsely decorated flat.

Everything about it and her unnerves me.

This is where she lives with her parents? It looks too small for two bedrooms. A dining-room table repels the hungry; a forlorn sofa slouches against a wall, and crumbs invite ants to nibble on the kitchen floor.

"Cup of tea?" she asks.

"We just had tea."

"I know, but I can't think of any other reason to keep you here."

"Just ask," I tell her with a kindness I do not feel.

"Won't Farah mind that you are in the flat of a beautiful woman?"

"Very much. Won't your fiancé mind?"

"He's probably seducing some girl right now."

"Is that what you're trying to do to me? Do you sleep with every available guy because that's what you think your fiancé does with every pretty girl? Is that why you wanted to join our discussion group?"

"No, I want you to make love to me because I'm frightened of terrorists, and I'm ashamed to admit that I'm scared."

"And here I thought you wanted me to seduce you because I'm so handsome."

"I really wanted to see if I can make you forget all about Farah."

"Put on the telly and let's see if we can find out whom the authorities want to blame for the attacks in the train station and Trafalgar Square."

"And you say I'm cynical?" she laughs.

As we watch the BBC broadcaster describe the horrific disaster and watch the ambulances carry away the victims she mutters, "Dumb terrorists, what do they think they'll accomplish? Do they think their murders are a valid political statement?"

"Perhaps we should tell them about Gandhi."

"Yeah, right. He won independence for India from Britain, and his own people killed him. Martyrdom doesn't suit the IRA. They use terror to gain their ends."

She walks over to the window, opens it and screams, "Shut up!"

"Whom are you yelling at?"

"That damn dog that belongs to the couple next door. Don't you hear him barking?"

"No, but he's probably terrified by the bomb blasts and the ambulance sirens. I can still hear the alarms."

"He barks all the time; he drives me nuts. I can't stand the way those people treat him."

"What do they do to him that's so horrible? Why don't you report them?"

"Report them? Yeah, I should report them to the insane asylum. They are always petting him, walking him up and down the street, putting sweaters on him when it's cold, and buying him steak. Imagine steak! Once I saw the man give him some beef, and then eat from exactly the same place that the dog just bit. The woman is worse; she constantly kisses the mutt on his forehead."

"Does he kiss her back?" I laugh.

"Ugh, he licks her nose after he's smelled all the other dogs' pee in the neighborhood. About ten of the mongrels congregate every morning and evening at the 'pee tree,' sniff each other's butts, lift their hind legs and baptize the area. It's a wonder the oak is still alive."

"Apparently, you don't like dogs."

"You do?"

"Not especially, but I know someone who did."

"Why would anyone like a dog?"

"She said that it was easy to love someone who loved her. And the dog really loved her. In fact, she continued to love it after it died."

"That's beyond stupid."

"No, she said people don't stop loving someone just because he died."

"But a dog isn't a person. And anyhow, dogs, according to Tolstoy, have no souls."

"Perhaps fools can be more profound than Tolstoy."

"You sound like you care for this girl and her dead dog."

"Don't you love someone who died?" I ask.

Nuzhat looks at me bitterly, "I don't even love anyone who's alive. Do you?"

"My brother died two years ago in an accident, and it was my fault. And yes, I love him dearly. I think about him constantly."

"Are you sure you feel love for him or guilt over the accident, which wasn't your fault?"

"How do you know it wasn't my fault?"

She turns away from me and murmurs, "I just assumed you wouldn't be the kind of person who would accidently kill someone you loved."

She knows that I know she has made a mistake. Suddenly, I realize that I never told her Farah's name and she's said it twice. I also realize I never should have mentioned even indirectly how Rebecca felt about dogs. So MI6, the Mossad, or Egyptian Intelligence is spying on me. But to send such a rank amateur indicates either that any one of those agencies is full of bunglers, or I am too far down on their list of priorities to rate a more professional agent tailing me.

"I think the terrorists have made enough social commentary for the day and the rain is letting up," I say as I look out the window. *Is there a man without a dog standing behind the "pee tree" looking up at her flat or am I paranoid?*

Paranoia keeps spies alive.

"So, I will not be seduced today?" she smiles. She has a horrible smile.

"I don't feel like being the victim of an honor-killing by an angry male relative."

"Trust me, no one cares enough about my honor to kill you."

"I don't know whether to be relieved about my safety or sad that no one cares about you."

She regards me thoughtfully. "You're a real romantic. That's dangerous, you know."

"Maybe for a political scientist. Not for someone who's studying the economic effects of the Nile River. Rivers are very romantic. Therefore, Egypt must dam her water. Then emotions can no longer flood her land."

"Your metaphors are terrible. Never become a poet."

"I promise. I'm not even a good economist. See you in class."

I leave the flat and have the feeling that the man behind the oak tree follows me all the way to my home, but every time I cautiously look behind me I see only shadows of buildings, trees, and clouds.

To protect Rebecca, I must avoid the longing I feel for her, and now I stay away from almost everyone except Henry. I diplomatically decline any more invitations to tea with Nuzhat; by the beginning of March she no longer attends class or returns to our group. I'm sure she'll be demoted by whichever agency hired her.

In late March, however, I strike up a friendship with an engaging Lebanese Christian student named Akram Al Hariri who lived in New York for the last ten years.

An international law student at Columbia University, Akram is spending a year in England studying the British judicial system. The young Lebanese, after a night of drinking in a pub, confides to me that he has fallen in love with a Jewish girl from Manhattan who is also studying law at Columbia.

"We decided to see how a year's separation will affect us. If we still feel the same way about each other when I'm through with my studies here, we are going to get married," Al Hariri says. "But after being away from her for three months I know I want to spend the rest of my life with her. Don't think I'm overly sentimental or an infatuated romantic, but Judy is the only girl I will ever love. If I didn't need these courses for my degree, I would have left London weeks ago."

"How do her parents feel toward you?" I ask him.

"She hasn't told them about us. She figured there's no point in upsetting them until I return. What she's really doing is buying peace for another nine months. My parents, of course, will disown me. They will say I am betraying my people and my faith. I know that for sure."

"And despite all this you're willing to marry her?"

"I'm not marrying my parents or hers. We will forge our own life together. In New York it's possible for all races to live together. There's a good reason New York is called the melting pot of the world. Let me tell you what it's like there," he says earnestly.

He takes a long sip of beer and leans back in his chair. "In my building an Indian Hindu family lives harmoniously across the hallway from Pakistani Muslims. Filipino doctors work together with Jews at Mount Sinai Hospital where my uncle is being treated for a rare blood disorder. In the restaurant a Frenchman talks to an Italian waiter in Spanish, the one language they all understand. Once, as I waited for my aunt to meet me at the entrance to the huge Macy's Department Store on 34th Street I saw women from at least thirty different ethnic groups barreling through the doors to take advantage of an after-Christmas sale. The women had different skin colors, believed in different religions, and spoke different tongues but they were all united in one goal: the almighty bargain!

"Americans don't care what race or religion you are," he asserts. "They just want to know how much money you have.

"In New York, Chinatown is next to Little Italy. Greek restaurants line 9th Avenue while Jews sell diamonds on 47th Street as Irish cops patrol Broadway. Judy and I can send our children to the School for Ethical Culture and forge a new kind of ecumenical awareness. Perhaps we can do away with prejudice and hatred. We will make a new kind of mind-set in the world."

This guy is a drunken idiot, I think to myself. *Is he so naive that he doesn't know about the friction between the Hispanic and Caucasian gangs? Is he blind to the animosity between the blacks and whites? Does Akram only see what he wants to see: a place where his Jewish fiancée and he could escape the pull of their disparate cultures, where they could disappear into the anonymity of the teeming city, where they could divorce themselves from the interminable warfare between Arab and Jew? How can he imagine a life in which the past has no bearing upon their future, and ancient animosities are forgotten?*

Then Akram proudly declares, "Columbia University asked me what nationality I was and required me to indicate if I am white, Hispanic, or black on a student questionnaire. I wrote, 'Like everyone else on this planet, I am an earthling.' I even started a campaign to make the school eliminate that question on its census form."

I can only admire the young Lebanese's earnestness and idealism even though he is a fool.

But then again, so am I.

I am amused by the young man's visionary aspirations and naiveté, and I wonder why Akram chooses to confide in me. It can't only be that he is often very drunk, passionately in love, and extremely indiscreet.

Although I have never told him about my relationship with Rebecca, I began to wonder if my own feelings about her are so transparent that even Akram is aware that I once made love to a Jewish woman. I examine every word I have ever said to the young law student, and I decide that Akram talks so freely to me because I am a very good listener and an extremely poor conversationalist. Although I am part of the circle of young Arabs who discuss politics, I seldom venture an opinion about any of the controversial topics of the day.

I must be cautious not to do so to avoid drawing any attention to myself. I surmise my silence has led the young Christian to believe that I am not a fervent Arab nationalist and might sympathize with his romantic involvement with a Jewish woman.

Al Hariri's passion is infectious, and against my better judgment, I allow the young man to become close to me. I'm weary of feeling so isolated and lonely; thus I'm extremely receptive to the friendship he offers me. I encourage him to confide in me. He tells me with great enthusiasm that his marriage will be the beginning of a new world order.

As I listen to the young Christian's dreams I can only hope that his and Judy's marriage will be a success. But I know that in the harsh world that separates cruel reality from idealistic daydreams, ethnic prejudices and religious intolerance will crush his naïve idealism. His dreams, like the dreams of all romantics, are doomed.

As spring begins to lighten the dismal, damp London streets, I become more and more depressed. Every contact I have with Henry makes me feel even more despondent. Then suddenly, after a meeting with the double agent, I realize that he is no longer disseminating any important information to me to relay to Egypt. Nor is he revealing undercover diplomatic activities between England, France, and America. Does he doubt my loyalty?

Henry knows I never wanted to be a soldier. I'm convinced Omar told him what happened to me while I was training my men in the desert. Can he tell I hate being an intelligence officer? Does he know I detest being in England? He's no idiot. I've been too noncommittal. Since the fiasco with Ken Philby and his Cambridge conspirators, Henry trusts no one.

And then paranoia overwhelms me. *Henry changed when I became friends with Akram. Akram constantly jaws on and on about Judy. Henry must be suspicious of me because I'm friendly with a Christian Arab who loves a Jew. Or even worse, Akram is a spy himself and fed me that whole story about being in love with a Jewess to try to lure me into revealing my feelings about Rebecca. Even though I never once mentioned her, maybe I gave myself away with a look, a gesture, an expression. Intelligence officers mislead everyone, especially their colleagues.*

I begin to view everyone with misgivings and doubt. Because I deceived the one person I love, I am sure that everyone is betraying me. I know there are many moles in the intelligence agency besides the Cambridge Five. Double agents proliferate at every level of the government. *How could I trust Akram? Why did I become involved in military intelligence? Why did I begin a life I never wanted? Why do my people have to hate Rebecca's? Why? Why? Why?*

Disloyalty to one's country brings about blessings and curses. It is a unified cycle of treachery. Only idiots trust each other.

In early spring, the rain falls continuously for weeks. The weather matches my mood.

"Oh to be in Egypt now that April's here," I jokingly remark to Henry one morning while I open a letter from my mother. Henry and I are meeting for a cup of steaming hot tea in a restaurant near the university. The letter contains news that makes me realize I must return to Cairo sooner than Intelligence originally planned.

"Edward, can you arrange for me to go home immediately?"

"Why?"

"My mother writes that my father is seriously ill with an inoperable intestinal tumor. The doctors do not know how much time he has left. He could last a few months or even a year or two. Not only does she want me to come home to see him before he dies, but she also wants me to fulfill his greatest wish, which is to marry the daughter of his dearest friend, General Fahey."

"I'm sorry about your father. I'll speak to the department about getting you leave to go home at once. Should I congratulate or commiserate with you about your impending wedding?"

"Careful, Henry. Don't ever joke about my fiancée or my personal affairs."

" Ishmael, I didn't mean…"

"I've known Farah for years. Our families are very close. I always knew I would marry her; our families have taken it for granted ever since we were teenagers. I just didn't think it would be so soon. But my father's illness changes everything. I know what my mother is thinking. She hopes that plans for my wedding and the possibility that my wife will conceive a son immediately will be enough impetus to keep my father alive, at least until he can hold his first grandson in his arms."

"Women are like that. They cling to every hope, no matter how far-fetched."

"My mother was eighteen when she married my father. She's enjoyed tremendous prestige as the wife of General Mohammed; in fact, being married to him is the only life she's ever known. If I give her a daughter-in-law and a grandson to fuss over, I can relieve some of the emptiness she'll experience if he dies."

"Won't your wife resent that?"

"No, Farah adores my mother. And my mother told me once that the best present I could ever give her would be to make Farah my wife. My children and my wife will be petted and spoiled, and they will pet and spoil my mother in return."

"Lucky guy. They'll treat you like a king when you come home."

"I am only sorry that my children may never know their grandfather. He is one of the great Egyptian patriots from a long line of illustrious generals. I always feel that I have failed him by not being in a fighting unit."

Henry raised his cup of tea. "To your father. To your wife."

I lift my cup, clink it against his, and join him in his insincere toast. Henry is such a bastard. He sees through me, and I hate him for that.

I try to remember the last private conversation I had with Farah and can't. All I recall is exchanging pleasantries with a tall, dark-eyed, fairly pretty girl with a long nose that stops just short of being unattractive. Fortunately, her high cheekbones and wide forehead prevent her nose from dominating her sweet face. Her winning smile and quiet manner, not her looks, are the qualities that first attracted her to me. Naturally, my father wants the match because Farah's father, a general in the army, is one of his best friends.

Her mother and mine vaguely knew that their husbands were colleagues and met at our tennis club. They decided to play in a doubles tournament, won the championship, and became best friends.

My father and Farah's were quite pleased that their wives were so compatible, and they decided that Farah and I should marry to further cement the relationship between the two families. I knew it would be useless to protest, and I could see that Farah had been raised to be a submissive, obedient daughter. I wanted to tell my parents that they have more in common with each other than Farah and I ever will. They should marry each other and leave us alone.

Life with Farah will be calm and passionless. She will be a docile, socially correct, and pleasant companion who will always defer to me in every important matter. What more can a husband want? My father only wants one thing: a grandson who will carry on the family name and the family military traditions. Our mothers' friendship now will be firmly cemented by the marriage.

And I love Rebecca!

I quickly calculate that if I leave London now I have enough time to visit Israel before I'm due in Cairo. I will convince Rebecca that both of us can leave the Middle East and forge a future for ourselves in New York devoid of both our countries' problems.

Perhaps Akram Al Hariri is right. At any rate, I will give it a try. Feverishly, foolishly, I make all sorts of ridiculous plans. I think of convincing arguments which I believe will persuade Rebecca to come with me. My excessive emotions are so neurotic that I am blind to all rational thoughts. Loyalties to Egypt, to Islam, to my family are traps which prevent me from being with the woman I love. The woman who is my enemy. A woman who belongs to a country who has stolen my family's home from us.

"Hear O Israel, Allah is one, Allah is our God, and He is not yours."

How can I love such a woman? How can I entreat her to follow me and make her God my God and make my people her people?

On my last day in London, I pass a tea shop on the way to the bus which is to take me to Heathrow Airport. By chance I glance in the window and am astounded to see Henry with his back to the street earnestly talking to Al Hariri, who also does not notice me. Their postures are intense; their faces scheming.

Apocalypse now! Forget seeing Rebecca!

I go into the tea shop and say goodbye to both of them. Akram congratulates me on my upcoming marriage. Are they uncomfortable that I have found the two of them together? I look at their faces, which are devoid of any emotion, accept their well wishes, and pretend not to be surprised that they know each other. Suddenly, I realize that since I told Henry I was returning to Cairo to marry Farah, Akram stopped talking about his Jewish girlfriend. The business of the whole world is to deceive the whole world!

But then, Philby and the rest of the Cambridge traitors schemed against the British government on far more serious matters, and the government knew exactly what they were doing and tracked them constantly. Are Henry, Nuzhat, and Akram working together? I don't give a damn. But I can't endanger Rebecca.

I must return to Cairo, marry Farah, and settle down to a desk job while my father begins the long, slow, painful process of dying. He listens to Nasser daily incite the Arab world to destroy Israel, to declaim that the Zionists caused all of Egypt's and Gaza's social and economic problems, and to encourage Muslims to kill Jews. I see little school children subjected to the most virulent anti-Semitic propaganda in schools where hatred, vengeance, and retaliation are taught more skillfully than reading, writing, and arithmetic. To contradict any of these practices and beliefs could mean jail or worse for my family. So, I keep quiet and maintain an outward façade that advocates the government's policies while inwardly I endure psychological turmoil.

I remember how much Simon, David, Rebecca, and Hannah wanted a homeland, a land where David joked that the Jews would finally have a land of their own. The newsboys, the farmers, even the gangsters would be Israelis. I saw many Jews with numbers tattooed on their arms; these Jews had survived horrendous atrocities, but had lost their fathers, mothers, brothers, sisters and children in a holocaust that many Arabs deny happened. I can still picture Rebecca's face when she told me that Simon and his family had buried the bars of soap made from the fat of Jews killed in Auschwitz.

Her account of the woman Gestapo officer who had a pair of earrings made from the beautiful eyes of a Jewish girl, and, of course, the story of Rebecca's necklace haunts me still. When the head of Egyptian military intelligence in Gaza and the Sinai is accidently killed by "friendly" fire in a fedayeen raid, I relive the attack on the beach in Ashkelon when Danny O'Halloran was riddled by bullets.

But I also must keep my promise to my mother who lost her home in Jerusalem, a home her family had lived in for many generations in a land ruled by her cousin, the Grand Mufti; the place where I spent some of the happiest days of my childhood visiting my cousins. I think of all the Palestinian refugees living in execrable camps under pitiable conditions. Their hope to return to their homeland is as great as the hope of the Jews.

And I know how the Jews love Jerusalem. It is their spiritual home away from home. If they are not in the holy city, they face in its direction when they pray. Every Passover, they vow that they will celebrate the holiday next year in this sacred place.

The Christians went on numerous crusades for it since their Christ died and was resurrected there. They sing hymns to the city for Christ's sake. They are waiting for their Messiah to return to it.

Our great prophet Mohammed ascended to Heaven from this holy site. Our Dome of the Rock is one of our most sacred mosques. My cousin General Abad El Kadar died defending Jerusalem from the Israelis.

Shared aspirations of each culture will bring despair to all.

Once a homeland is abandoned, exiles love it even more than they did when they inhabited it. Collective dreams turn into nightmares for the dispossessed.

I cannot bear to disappoint my family or be disloyal to the Arabs and Islam. Yet, I feel that in serving them I am betraying the only woman I can ever love. If I do not betray her, I defame my people, my country, my religion, my father, and destroy my mother's dream.

I marry Farah.

My parents are happy.

I feel as if I will go mad.

My father's tumor responds to treatment, and he waits impatiently to cradle his first grandson in his arms as Farah, the perfect wife, becomes pregnant two months after our marriage.

I pretend to be the dutiful husband.

Omar's constant shadow over me ensures that I will never do anything to damage my career or harm my family's reputation.

In February of 1958, I manage to become part of a delegation going to Syria to establish the United Arab Republic which Nasser and the Syrian President Shukri al Quawati want to form to resist a communist takeover of the region.

After the ceremonial signing I convince my colleagues that I should investigate the northern Israeli settlements near the Syrian border in the shadow of the Golan Heights. Conflicts on this border have been common since 1949, and I persuasively argue that if I could discover information about Israeli forces and artillery locations in this area I would enable our new allies to wipe out these settlements.

I don an Israeli army uniform, rent a car, and drive to several border villages. I walk around a few settlements, take a few pictures, drink a great deal of coffee, and then drive south to Ashkelon. Discretion makes me go first to the café that I frequented with Rebecca and her family instead of driving by her home.

I sit at the familiar outdoor table and order a coffee. I am so saturated with caffeine and so agitated that I expect to see Omar sitting at a nearby table.

When the waitress brings the cup to me I casually ask her if she knows Rebecca Silverman.

"You mean Rebecca Neuwirth. She married after the 1956 Suez War."

"Married! Whom did she marry?"

"Simon Neuwirth. They were childhood friends."

"But I thought Simon was going to marry her sister, Hannah."

"Hannah and David both died in the war. Didn't you know that?" the waitress asks me. Then, as she sees the stunned expression on my face, she says gently, "I guess you didn't."

I try to control the tremor in my voice as I ask, "Does Rebecca, do the Neuwirths, live here in Ashkelon?"

"No, I heard she and Simon moved to Tel Aviv. Her parents and Simon's still live here though."

I manage to say, "Thanks for the coffee." I throw two liras on the table and hastily leave.

I can imagine the look of surprise on the waitress's face when she sees that I have left a tip worth four times the cup of coffee I ordered.

I am so confused and stunned that I no longer care what mistakes I make. Hannah and David dead! Rebecca and Simon married!

How could I be so naive as to think she would spend the rest of her life waiting for me when I never bothered to keep in touch with her? She probably thought I seduced her and then abandoned her.

But why did she marry Simon? I remember Rebecca telling me she thought that Simon was the handsomest boy in Ashkelon. She must have been secretly in love with Simon all the time. Once Hannah died she probably jumped at the chance to marry him. I stride up the street in a state of feverish, jealous anger for a few blocks. Then I calm down somewhat and began to think sensibly for the first time in a year.

No, she wasn't secretly in love with Simon. She did love me. Simon did love Hannah. She thought I deserted her. Since Simon couldn't marry Hannah, he probably wanted to be with the one person who was closest to her. How could I not have written to her? Why hadn't I explained myself to her earlier?

You crazy idiot, Ishmael. You know why you didn't write to her. You deliberately ended your future with her when you left Israel. How could you imagine that she would even consider marrying you if she knew the truth about you? Did you really think she would forsake her family, her country, her religion, and marry you?

I suddenly realize I'm muttering so wildly to myself in Arabic that people in the street begin to look at me oddly. In my distracted state I'm scarcely conscious of the attention I'm attracting until I notice several women staring at me in alarm. With difficulty I compose myself, smile at the ladies reassuringly, and quickly turn around and walk back to the spot across from the café where I had parked my rental car. I open the door, sit down in the driver's seat and take a deep breath.

Gripping the steering wheel I think, *I haven't been rational ever since I received the telegram from my mother. I don't want to go through the façade of a marriage with Farah. I don't want to be a general. I don't want to work in military intelligence. I don't want to do what everyone in my family expects me to do."*

Destiny destroys dreams.

I slowly insert the key into the ignition and start the engine. With a sigh I begin the long drive back to Syria. As I arrive at the outskirts of Tel Aviv I become obsessed with an overwhelming desire to see Rebecca one more time before I leave Israel. I stop at a corner telephone booth and thumb through the directory until I find the name Neuwirth, Simon. I note with relief that the Neuwirths' street address is listed along with the telephone number. I find the street quickly in my pocket map of the city and drive there without too much difficulty. I park across the street from the house that has a small flower garden in the front yard and wait. I don't know what I will do if I see her. My mind is racing with all sorts of fantasies that I know are not logical. In fact, at that moment, sitting in front of her house, I am quite irrational. I have immense sympathy for every neurotic, overwrought, revolutionary romantic who ever existed.

I could easily murder Simon Neuwirth.

About 15 minutes later I see her walking with Simon toward the house, and my fantasies evaporate in an instant. Rebecca is pushing a baby in a stroller, and Simon and she are laughing and talking as they come up the street. The baby is sucking contentedly on a pacifier and waving its little hands in the air. As I gaze at the three of them, I feel a pang of envy and realize how foolish my feelings for her are. All my dreams are really disordered nightmares of fierce vexation, intolerable longings, conflicted loyalties, and an impossible love.

I watch Rebecca take the baby out of the stroller and cradle it in her arms as she waits for Simon to walk up the steps and unlock the door to their house. Quickly, without thinking, I grab my camera and take a picture of her as she holds the baby, their baby. Wretchedly, I see Simon take the child from her and carry him? her? up the steps. I watch enviously as Simon waits at the threshold for Rebecca to precede him into the house. He shuts the door behind them with a finality that will reverberate irrevocably in my memory.

After they have gone into the house I feel as though I am walking across the Tower Bridge in London and the drawbridge has suddenly opened, plunging me down, down, down, down into the fast-flowing Thames. I had read that an American policeman driving on a similar drawbridge fell into the Intracoastal Waterway in Florida when a watchman forgot to lower the barrier pole as the roadway opened. I wondered if the unfortunate victim, trapped in his car as it toppled into the murky river, felt as hopeless and anguished as I did when I saw Simon, Rebecca, and their child go into the house, and I heard the front door slam shut against the outside world.

I start the car's engine and drive toward Damascus. I will become the career intelligence agent my father and father-in-law expect me to become. For my father's sake I will make the brilliant career moves that will earn me a general's star. But I vow that I will never pressure any of my sons to become a general; nor will I arrange a marriage for any of my children. *My father dictates my life, I won't dictate my children's. But it isn't only my father,* I think grimly. *It's my whole damn history!*

I wonder if my father is happy. Did he want to become a general? Did he want to marry my mother?

I can't recall seeing my parents sharing any intimate, loving moments. My mother seems happy enough, but she spends more time with her women friends than she does with my father. *It's time to break the pattern*, I promise myself.

I return to Damascus, file a report on the northern Israeli border settlements, then fly back to Cairo. For the rest of my life I dutifully fulfill my family's expectations in every way except one. Much to my amusement and immense satisfaction, no child of mine will ever become an Egyptian army officer, for instead of giving my father the longed-for grandson, I will give him four lovely, long-nosed daughters.

Rebecca

WALKING SHADOWS

TEL AVIV 1965

Ghosts. Everywhere I look, I see ghosts. The unseen are seen. The dead walk in my dreams. They are desperate visions that stop time and bring back the ones I love. I hate visiting my parents' home because I see Hannah and David in every niche. This was the chair where David sat every night to eat his supper. There, Hannah would plop down on the floor to pet our dog Beggar. I hate every slim, graceful, reddish-blonde haired girl in a military uniform who is alive. I can't bear to look at any paratrooper who resembles David. How dare they be alive while my brother and sister are dead? I know Simon feels the same way; whenever we see someone who is similar to Hannah or David we silently exchange glances that question the vicissitudes of life.

I can never go again to Ashkelon's beach. Simon assumes it is because I am still traumatized by the fedayeen attack that caused Danny O'Halloran's death. How could I tell him it is because that was the place where for the first and last time I made love with Isaac? Over and over again I am haunted by the passion, the ecstasy, the sensual, and romantic fulfillment of that night.

I see Isaac each time I look at my oldest son's face. It is torment to be married to the man you like when you are constantly reminded of the man you love.

Simon named the child Isaac. Kindness or cruelty?

While our second son resembles my brother David, Simon is disappointed that our daughter does not have Hannah's reddish-blonde hair or perky personality. He will never know why.

Religious ritual, politics, and soccer occupy most of Simon's time. He adores our children, David and Hannah, treats me with all due respect, and is distantly kind to Isaac. Israel does not have a more devoted citizen. Soccer does not have a more fanatic fan. I could not have a more conscientious husband. Both of us hide our unfulfilled love for the ghosts in our lives from the children, from the world, and from each other.

I can't forget Isaac's father. Is he alive? Why did he never contact me after that moonlit night on the beach? Why could we never find any trace of him? Simon spent one week's pay calling Sandhurst to inquire about a Professor Ben Abraham. No one knew any professor at any college in England with the last name of Ben Abraham.

He called the camp Isaac had told us he was going to for basic training. Neither that base nor any other training camp in Israel had a recruit named Isaac Ben Abraham. Isaac disappeared into thin air and if I didn't have his son to remind me of him every minute of my life, I would think my nineteenth summer was nothing more substantial than a dream.

Often I wonder if I magnify my romantic feelings about the man I knew that summer because I was so young, so naive, so vulnerable. Was he really that good looking? Of course, he was. One glance at my son reminds me how handsome Isaac was. The child has his charisma, his charm, and his brilliance. When Isaac smiles at me, I see his father's ghost. When Isaac laughs, Simon frowns.

I don't want to believe his father seduced me and deceived all of us. Simon is sure that Isaac was a spy. I look at my son, and all I see is the man I once loved and still do.

Secrets whisper everywhere in our house. Ghosts never die.

Simon

TEL AVIV

1966

Each time I look at the child, I see the face of the man Rebecca loves. She lives only in the past. I live only in the present. Our future is based on remembering those whom we have lost.

I pretend not to notice that his voice, mannerisms, even his walk resembles his father's. His precociousness irritates me. He is so much brighter than our younger children. At the school picnic he won every race and was awarded a medal as best student of the year.

I never told my mother and father that Isaac is not their grandchild. He's the child of the man my wife loves. He's the son of a man who recited poetry, acted in Shakespearean plays, and wrote articles for *National Geographic*.

He's the child of a man who seduced a girl, and then abandoned her.

Abandoned or betrayed her?

Secrets whisper everywhere in our house.

Isaac Neuwirth

JERUSALEM

JUNE 1967

My father trumpets the horn on our little Ford and shouts jubilantly, "Isaac, get in the car. Uncle Yossi, you and I are going to Jerusalem, to the Western Wall."

"I'm waiting for Mom, David, and Hannah," I call to him.

"Mom is staying home with David and Hannah. Your brother and sister are too little to come with us. You are almost nine years old; this is a trip just for us men."

Then he invites me to sit between Uncle and him in the front seat which astounds me. Usually, Mom sits next to Dad. I always sit in the back with my little sister and brother. I have never seen him so excited or so proud and happy. He smiles at me the way he smiles at David and Hannah.

If Mom praises me because I get a 95 on a test, he wants to know why I didn't get a 100. If I earn a 100, he says that the test was so easy any fool could have gotten a perfect grade. I have a father whom I can never please, yet he never yells at Hannah and David. If they break a dish or take one of my toys, he says that's what little kids do, but I'm the oldest and I should know better. Sometimes, I think he hates me, especially when I won a race last month.

But today, he is all smiles and pleasant conversation. When we approach the Western Wall of the Second Temple and join the enthusiastic crowd that throngs the walkway, he puts his arm around my shoulder, and I feel that he really does love me.

Together we go up to the wall and touch it. I see some people are putting little pieces of paper in the cracks between the stones.

"What are they doing, Papa?"

"Sending letters to God."

"How will God get those letters?"

"The spirit of God is in this place, Isaac. You must defend this place with your life. Your uncle David died so we could begin to get it back from the Arabs. All your ancestors going back thousands of years to the first Isaac worshipped God, and this is the place where He lives. That is why Uncle Yossi and I brought you here. Never forget that. Swear that you won't."

"I will never forget, Papa, I swear."

Someone in the crowd begins singing "Jerusalem of Gold" and we join in. Soon everyone in the plaza is singing the chorus, and I have never been so proud to be an Israeli. In the distance is a domed shaped building with a golden roof which gleams in the sunlight. I have never seen such a beautiful place. I point to it and ask, "Papa, is that why we say Jerusalem is the golden city? Let's go to that building. That must be where God is."

My father gives me a look that is awful in its cruel intensity. I know immediately that I have said something terribly wrong. I start to tremble and want to ask him what I said that upset him; I want the papa back that I had a moment ago, but I dare not question him. He takes his arm off my shoulder and glares at the golden dome. He and Uncle Yossi look at each other strangely. Then he scowls at me.

"Do you know what that place is?" he asks in a voice that terrifies me.

"It has a gold roof, Papa. Are you mad at me because it looks like an onion, and God would never live in any building that has a roof shaped like an onion?"

Papa looks severely at me for a long minute, but Uncle Yossi begins to laugh. Papa, however, still looks angry. What did I say that upset him so much? Why is Uncle laughing?

Then Papa stoops down and looks directly into my eyes. He is always so serious, but I have never seen him look at me so sternly before.

"I am not mad at you, Isaac. But you are right. God does not live in that building. Our enemies live there. They erected that building in our holiest place to spite us. We just fought a war against them because they would not let us visit this wall where God does live. They would take this wall back if they could. They would take all of Israel away from us. That is why I want you to swear that you will defend Jerusalem and never let them take it away from us again. Promise me."

"I promise. I will protect Jerusalem forever and ever. I will protect you, Uncle Yossi, Momma, David, and Hannah from them, too."

Papa smiles and puts his arm around me again. I am so glad he likes me once more.

Rebecca

ON THE ROAD TO ASHKELON

May 1979

I shmael hands me another picture. I glance at a photo of myself and my two younger children walking in a street in Tel Aviv and exclaim, "When did you take this?"

"About 14 years ago. After our last night together I was sent directly to Cairo and was posted to England a few days later. I didn't return to Egypt for almost 2 years. While I was in London I did not dare to ask anyone about you. I was afraid that if I made inquiries, Egyptian Intelligence would suspect that I really cared about you. They deduced that I did and tried to entrap me. If they had succeeded, both of us would have been in grave danger.

"Two years later I returned to Ashkelon and made a few discreet inquiries. I was absolutely dumbfounded when I learned you were married to Simon, had one child, and lived in Tel Aviv. I had always nurtured the romantically ridiculous notion that you and I could somehow have a life together. I was told that if I wanted to find Hannah I should go to the cemetery. And I heard how David died."

"I was frantic when you didn't come to David's memorial service. At first, I thought you, too, had died. Then I began to think that you had deceived all of us, and I blamed you for David's and Hannah's deaths. I became so paranoid that I tortured myself with the ridiculous idea that somehow you had acquired the plans for the deployment of David's unit in the Sinai and warned the Egyptian army."

"How you must hate me."

"You mean you did warn the Egyptians?"

"I gave the Egyptian High Command plans of an operation called 'Hand of Samson' which detailed how the Israelis would attack Egypt through the Sinai Peninsula. It was my job, Rebecca."

I turn from him and stare blindly through the window. A visceral thrust of the truth I've always subliminally known instantly destroys the idolized delusions I had of a lover who never really existed. All the despair and grief I had accumulated ever since he abandoned me turn instantly into feelings of anger and revenge.

"Rebecca," he says softly, "what would you have done if you were in my place, and you knew your country was going to be attacked?"

"You used me, you used David, Hannah, Simon, my uncle, all of us."

"At first. But then I fell in love with you. And I knew you would never love me if you knew who I really am."

"Why didn't you at least ask me?"

"I tried. Don't you remember your reaction when I said your necklace needed a Muslim crescent added to the Christian cross and the Star of David?"

"But that was hypothetical. I thought you were talking in general and making a joke."

"No, I was testing the waters."

I turn and look at him fiercely. "If the situation were reversed would you give up your religion, your country, and your family and become a Jew? Would you wear a Star of David?"

At that moment the taxi driver slams on the brakes and screams "Shit."

Everyone suddenly lurches forward, and the man next to Ishmael bangs his head on the back of the driver's seat. The cab screeches to a stop inches from a prostrate donkey lying in the center of the road. Standing over her and braying mournfully are three small foals. Everyone, including the injured passenger who is starting to grow a bump in the middle of his forehead, scrambles out of the car and goes over to the donkey, who is moaning piteously.

"Look there," says the taxi driver. He points to an ugly-looking gash under the donkey's right rib. "Someone must have hit her and didn't even stop. They just left her lying here. If it were nighttime I could have run right over the poor thing."

The injured Arab reaches inside a knapsack he's carrying and takes out a canteen of water. Slowly and gently, he pours the water into the wound. The foals stop their braying and solemnly watch him tend to their mother.

I take off the scarf I am wearing around my neck and bind the wound. "Look, the donkey is so thin the scarf reaches around her entire flank."

"You know," Ishmael says, "The ancient Canaanites worshipped a donkey god they called Palés."

"This little donkey mother was the object of worship?"

"She was sometimes a He. The ancient people of this area believed that Palés was a very mischievous fertility god and could change sexes at will. Anyone who wanted a child prayed to Palés, who might grant the wish if it suited his or her mood. Everybody thinks this country was named Palestine after the Philistines who lived in Gaza, Ashkelon, and a few other cities on the coast, but I wonder if it wasn't named after Palés. At any rate, donkeys were very important animals in the Middle East for thousands of years since they were the primary mode of transportation.

"But this donkey is in a very sorry state. I wonder why she is wandering on the highway. And with three babies yet!"

"What do we do with them?" asked the cab driver. "We just can't leave them here. She'll bleed to death and her foals will starve."

I jump at the sound of an indignant horn bearing down on us at breakneck speed. A pickup truck that seems to have no regard for any speed limit stops angrily inches from the rear end of the taxi. The burly driver leans belligerently out of his window. "What in Hell? You're blocking traffic."

Ishmael glares at him. Barely controlling his anger at the Israeli's rudeness, he is about to shout at the truck driver when I softly explain, "There's an injured animal on the road and we're just trying to figure out how to move her without causing her any further pain."

Instantly the man's expression softens. "Let me see," he offers. "Maybe I can help." He climbs out of his truck and examines the wounded donkey. Gently he palpates the area around the wound. The donkey moans and tries to move away from him. "I think her jaw is broken. And she has some lacerations to her flank as well. If you help me put a blanket under her we can lift her into the back of my pickup."

"What will you do to her?" I ask anxiously.

"Take X-rays of her jaw and flanks, give her antibiotics and cleanse and dress her wounds and wire the jaw if it's broken. We'll also feed the youngsters. I'll bet they're still nursing, and Momma is in no condition to tend to them."

"Are you a veterinarian?" asks Ishmael.

"No, but I live at Kibbutz Issachar near here, and I often help our vet with our farm animals. Donkeys are very special to us, and we have a nice little herd."

"Why are donkeys so special to your kibbutz?" Ishmael asks.

The burly truck driver shrugs. "When we first started our kibbutz we were so poor we couldn't afford horses. So some of us went out into the desert and rounded up some wild donkeys. They weren't as hard to tame as horses, and those of us who were not too fat rode them."

"What did the fat people do?" Ishmael asks.

"Oh, they loaded their stuff on the donkeys and walked beside them. After they walked for a month or two they weren't so fat anymore. Now help me get this little momma and her babies into the truck."

I hold the foals while the four Muslims help the Israeli slide a blanket under the wounded donkey. Then he lowers the back panel and places a ramp on the truck bed that leads to the ground. Each man gently lifts an edge of the blanket and together they carry the donkey up the ramp into the truck. I then help the truck driver lead the little ones into the pickup beside their mother. They immediately nuzzle her and she moans softly.

I give each of the baby donkeys a soft caress on the head and bend over the mother's neck and whisper, "You'll feel much better soon; the people on the kibbutz will take good care of all of you." Impatiently, the taxi and truck drivers simultaneously blast their horns at me signaling their desire to reach their destinations before sundown. With a last gentle pat to the injured donkey's head I reluctantly leave the truck and reenter the cab.

"You're right. I couldn't," said Ishmael.

"Couldn't what?"

"Remember what you asked me before the cab driver slammed on his brakes and avoided causing more harm to the injured donkey and her babies? You wanted to know if I could give up my country and religion. Yet I was going to ask you to do that when I came back to look for you. I was going to tell you who I really was and ask you to marry me. You have no idea how I felt when I learned you had married Simon and had a child."

"As I just told you, I thought you were dead. Then when Simon learned that you never contacted me again he saved me."

"What do you mean 'saved' you?'

"Don't you know why Simon married me so quickly?"

"That has always puzzled me. No, it did more than that. It destroyed me; it ripped me apart. I thought his love for Hannah must have been as shallow as your love for me. How could he have forgotten Hannah so quickly? How little did I mean to you? Did the funeral meats furnish the wedding table?"

"Stop with the Shakespearean allusions. Stop feeling sorry for yourself. People don't necessarily marry for love. Sometimes a man chivalrously marries a woman to rescue her and her unborn child from dishonor and shame."

"Unborn child?"

"Our child!"

Ishmael stares at me in amazement, "You mean your oldest child is my son?"

"Yes, his name is Isaac. You know, we Jews often name our children after a close dead relative to honor his or her memory. So I named him after the name I knew his father by. I named him for a person who never really existed. What a laugh!"

"Why do you say that? What is there to laugh about?"

"The name Isaac means 'she laughed.' The biblical Sarah could not believe the angels who told her she was going to have a child in her old age so she laughed when she heard the prophecy."

"But we made love only once!"

"Well, I read somewhere that if you are married you have to make love many times, in Sarah's case, many years, until you can have a baby. But if you're not married, you only have to make love once. Isn't that a funny joke Palés played on me?"

Ishmael does not laugh. I can see he is in shock, and I am glad.

"So you only married Simon to give my son a name?"

"He's still in love with Hannah, and he knows how I felt about you. I think he married me as a way to stay as close as he could to Hannah and David. And he cares for me as deeply as he is able. We have two children of our own, and he treats Isaac well enough. In fact, Simon was with Colonel Gur's 55th Parachute Brigade when Israel won all of Jerusalem in the 1967 War, and his proudest moment as a father was when he took Isaac as soon as possible to pray with him at the Western Wall."

"It was my fault that Israel won the war with Jordan."

"Your fault?"

"I told Nasser to tell the Jordanian king that most of the Israeli air force had been destroyed when, in reality, the Egyptian force was totally wiped out. I also told our Field Marshall Amer to inform King Hussein that the Egyptian army was already across the Negev and would soon reach Hebron. The Iraqis were supposed to tell him that they had bombed Tel Aviv, and the Syrians promised to send support for the war within a week.

"You set up King Hussein?"

"We lied like hell. Not only we Egyptians, but also the Iraqis and the Syrians betrayed him. He lost half his kingdom and never trusted us again."

"Why did you do that?'

"There was hysteria in the region. We wanted Israel destroyed, but Nasser did not want to lose another war against Israel. He could not lose face among the Arabs. Our intelligence informed us that Jordan could easily defeat Israel. We were wrong. I was wrong.

He turns and looks at me. "That's not the real reason. I was born in Jerusalem. I wanted to be able to take my mother back to her home. It had been in her family for hundreds of years. It was her dream to reclaim it, and I used subterfuge, lies, and deceit to try to win it back for her. Imagine how it feels to lose your home and then regain it."

I give him a withering glare. "I can't imagine how it feels. After all, we Jews lost our homes only 2,000 years ago. How many holocausts and genocides did your mother's family endure in the last 19 years? How many people have denied that holocausts have ever taken place against your people? How many..."

"Look, we could go on forever trading tales of atrocities each of our cultures has suffered. We know them only too well. Tell me about my son."

"He does not know that Simon is not his biological father. Both Simon and I thought that knowledge would destroy him. Can you imagine how he would feel if he knew the truth? He has an identity. Don't destroy it. Family, country, and religion have given him his sense of self. Please, don't reveal to him who you are. Two years ago he graduated from Flight Training School, and now he is a jet fighter pilot in the Israeli Air Force. If he found out his father was not Simon, but an Arab general in Egyptian Military Intelligence who may have been responsible for his uncle's and aunt's deaths he would be devastated."

"So you're doing to him what your parents did to Hannah."

"We tell lies to protect the truth. Imagine if your whole life you believe you know who you are. You know who your parents, your native country, your religion, your background is. You are certain where your loyalties lie." I look at him fiercely, "If we told Hannah her parents were not only Christian, but Polish, she might have been bewildered and shocked, but we know Simon would subconsciously hold it against her, even though he loved and still does adore her. He thinks she was a sabra who died while fighting for her country. His illusions sustain him.

"Isaac has to work hard to win Simon's approval for everything. My husband always sees your face when he looks at the boy. Isaac knows that Simon favors the younger children; he knows he disappointed his father because he became a pilot instead of a paratrooper. He thinks Isaac is following in your footsteps through some genetic force."

Ishmael laughs, "That's ironic. I never wanted to be a pilot. I only said that to impress your uncle. I led an infantry unit in the army before I became an intelligence agent."

For a few minutes Ishmael does not say a word to me. In the distance a bird glides gracefully over the Mediterranean, its wing tips capturing the golden rays of the setting sun. Finally, he softly whispers, "Can I at least see him?"

"Haven't you seen him over the years?"

"No, I only searched for you. I thought the children were all Simon's, so I took no interest in them. Every time I saw you in Israel you were only with a little boy and girl."

"What do you mean 'every time you saw me in Israel'?"

"Before the '67 and '73 wars and whenever I had a special assignment I would always go to see you and take a picture of you."

"Why?"

"I thought if I died or was captured at least I had the chance to see you one more time. I also had the foolish idea that your picture would be my good luck charm, and nothing bad would happen to me."

"That's ridiculous and absurdly romantic."

"I know. But here are all the pictures I took. Funny, Isaac isn't in any of them."

"That's because you took the first few photos during school hours. Hannah and David were too little at that time to go to kindergarten. Why did you never speak to me before today? Have you been following me for years?"

"Forever. You always had a child, a friend, or Simon with you. Today is the first time I saw you without someone by your side. If you had run into the bus station, if a terrorist hadn't blown up the pizza parlor, I would never have had the chance to invite you into this cab."

"People had to die and my father had to break a leg so you could talk to me. Why did you become a spy? Why did you betray me?"

"I think every first-born son in my family for many generations has been a general in the Egyptian army. My father jokes that our oldest ancestor led Antony and Cleopatra's armies against Augustus Caesar. His great-grandfather served under Mohammed Ali Pasha and led his armies against Nubia, Crete, and Palestine. My own father served under Nasser."

"Ishmael, a general is not a spy."

"I know. When I graduated from Sandhurst I was given a commission as a second lieutenant and was put in charge of a group of raw recruits. One of them was my brother, Abdul, who had just enlisted. Abdul idolized me since he was a child. I was leading them into the desert on a training mission. No one realized that the supply truck that followed us had been slowly leaking oil for miles. When we stopped at a campsite to bivouac I went ahead to scout out the next day's hiking route.

"One of the soldiers, against orders, started to smoke in the evening twilight and tossed his burning cigarette stub on the ground. It landed on an oil slick and started a fire. Suddenly flames engulfed the entire camp. The boys tried desperately to put out the fire, but by the time I saw the light from the flames and ran back to camp, my brother's entire body was horribly burned and several others were badly injured. I thought if so many soldiers could die or be wounded on a training mission then I wanted no part of any actual fighting."

"So you thought you could avoid combat by becoming a spy."

"I requested a transfer to military intelligence. I disappointed my father, but he understood my reasons. And he saw me become a general before he died. But I still managed to fail him."

"How?" I ask bitterly. "You certainly performed well during the Suez War."

"My wife had four daughters. Each time she became pregnant he hoped she was bearing another general. And each time the child was a girl."

'"He may yet have a grandson who will be a general. But not in the Egyptian army."

Shocked, Ishmael stares at me. "It's a good thing my father is already dead. If not...if he would ever discover who the potential general in the family could be..."

"Irony is mine, sayeth the Lord. And how do you feel about it?"

Now Ishmael cannot look at me. Finally, he says with a sad little smile, "Do you remember that I told you once that I had acted in *Romeo and Juliet*?"

"Yes, I think you said you were the prince."

"Right. And I believe I had the most important lines in the play. Have you ever seen it?"

"Years ago. And I can't remember any great lines that the prince said."

"No one does. But when I first read them I thought that they were the most powerful lines in all of Shakespeare. My jaw actually dropped because I wondered how anyone could sum up the theme of the entire play in four lines. Later, I thought that these words summed up everything that happened to us and I cannot tell you how often I say them to myself. Now, they have more meaning for me than ever."

"What lines are they?"

"At the end of the play the grieving fathers of Romeo and Juliet stand behind their dead children's coffins at the joint funeral. The prince of Verona frowns despairingly at the anguished parents and says:

> See what a scourge is laid upon your hate,
> That heaven finds means to kill your joys with love.
> And I for winking at your discords too
> Have lost a brace of kinsmen. All are punish'd.

"But the prince only lost cousins. I have loved my country and hated her enemies. This love for Jerusalem killed what joy I could have had with the woman I love and with my son."

"And it ruined my love for you and killed my brother and Hannah, who should have been Simon's wife."

"We really are cursed by heaven, aren't we?" Ishmael whispers sadly.

"Do you really think it's heaven's fault?"

"No, I suppose not. But, Rebecca, suppose you had been in my position. Would you have acted any differently? Would you have put Israel in jeopardy because of your love for me?"

She stares at me, then looks away. "I'm glad the generals of Israel and the rabbis didn't ask me to betray you as the Philistine princes and priests asked Delilah to betray Samson. She acted just as you did. Would I have done the same? I don't know. Would I betray Israel if I told Isaac not to fight against the Arabs? How can I tell him that if he did, he might possibly kill his father and stepsisters? How can I tell him who his father really is, and why his father made love to me? I'm afraid it would make him hate you and all Arabs even more than he does now."

"Rebecca, when I made love to you it wasn't because I had devious intentions. It was because I truly and deeply cared for you. You must believe me. I knew I would not be able to see you again for a long time. But I had already determined that I would come back to you after the conflict was over, explain my circumstances to you, and ask you to come to Egypt with me and become my wife."

"And what would have happened to your career? How would your father, who was disappointed in his Egyptian daughter-in-law, act towards an Israeli one even if she did give him a grandson? No, no, don't you see marriage would have been impossible? Besides, my family would have been crushed. They would have disowned me, and the hurt our marriage would have caused would have been something I could never have inflicted upon them."

"My love for you would not overcome this?"

"You know it wouldn't. And if your love for me had been greater than your love for Egypt and Islam, you never would have left me in the first place. You never would have betrayed all of us. And I could never betray my country and my faith. Never!"

Just then, the taxi driver announces to Ishmael in Arabic that the cab is entering Ashkelon's city limits. I know enough of the language to understand that he wants to know if he should leave me off at the bus station. Ishmael answers him, and I gasp in astonishment when I see the cab pass by the terminal and wend its way toward my parents' home.

"You remember where I lived!"

"I remember everything about that summer."

The taxi draws up to the Silvermans' house and stops in front of it. Ishmael opens the door and waits for me to exit the car. The front door of my parents' home flies open and my son, our son, wearing the uniform of an Israeli Air Force jet pilot, comes bounding down the steps.

"Mom, where have you been? We were so worried because Dad told us you were taking the noon bus. When you weren't on it Grandma called Dad at his office, and he told us if you weren't on the bus he didn't know where you could be. Then we heard about the terrorist attack near the terminal. He's called the police who told us hundreds were injured and many were killed in the blast. He is getting ready to go to the bomb site to find out what happened to you. We'll phone him right now and tell him you came by cab."

Then my son stops in amazement when he sees that my taxi displays the green and white license plate of an Arab cab and that the other occupants are four Muslim men.

I am nervously aware of how intensely Ishmael is staring at him.

Before either one can say a word, I say to my son, "This gentleman is an old friend of our family who used to live in Ashkelon many years ago. When he saw that I missed the bus because of the terrorist attack, he generously offered to bring me here in his taxi since he and the other men are on their way to Gaza. He knew that if he didn't ask me to join them I would have no other way of coming here to help Grandma take care of Grandpa. And he assured me that he would guarantee my safety."

Isaac gravely extends his hand to Ishmael. "Thank you, sir, for seeing that my mother did arrive here unharmed."

Ishmael shakes his son's hand. "It was my pleasure. We had a most eventful journey."

"Not really," I interject before Ishmael can say another word. "We found an injured donkey on the highway, and luckily someone from a kibbutz came along and took her and her three babies to its vet in his truck. That's why we are so late."

I am aware that Isaac does not hear me. He is staring intently at Ishmael who does not let go of my son's hand. Ishmael's eyes are devouring every inch of his son's body for what seems to be an eon to me, and Isaac is gazing as intently at him.

Suddenly, a dark epiphany appears in Isaac's eyes as he sees himself reflected in Ishmael's face. Now he understands Simon's slights and coolness. Now the enormity of his heritage engulfs all of us. He looks at both of us with an unfathomable look. Ishmael and I know he immediately understands that we are all Fortune's Fools.

It took me a half hour to recognize Ishmael. But my son recognizes his father instantly, just as I knew who my real father was when I saw him in Yanek's home. Has Isaac always had his doubts about his relationship to Simon? Has he always felt the divisions between belonging and alienation, identity and isolation, enmity and amity? I cannot bear to look at either man. My son, my son, what have we done to you? What will you do to me, to us?

The taxi driver impatiently blows his horn and shouts at Ishmael in Arabic that it is getting late. I can see that the last thing he wants to do is get in the cab. "Give your mother a 'Shabbat Shalom' greeting from me and tell your father I hope his leg heals quickly," he murmurs to me, but he never takes his eyes away from his son's face. When the taxi driver beeps his horn again, he turns reluctantly and slowly walks toward the cab; each step is a deliberate retracing of past actions and present regrets.

Impulsively, I follow him to the car. As he opens the door to the taxi, he whispers to me, "It is a great disappointment never to have a son. It is worse to have a son and then lose him. When Tennyson wrote "it is better to have loved and lost than never to have loved at all' he had no idea how wrong he was."

He looks back at Isaac who has picked up my little overnight bag and is waiting tensely for me to accompany him into the house. Finally, Ishmael enters the taxi, much to the relief of the impatient driver and the other passengers. Taking one final all-devouring look at his son he suddenly reaches out of the window and grasps my hand warmly one last time and then resolutely relinquishes it. He settles into his seat and nods to the cab driver.

As the taxi rounds the corner he turns and gives us a final wave of his hand. I can picture him sitting in the car with his eyes tightly closed until the taxi reaches Gaza.

Epilogue

Palés

The Twilight of the Goddess

Kibbutz Issachar

Iwill never be worshipped again. My wounds are too deep. Abandoned by my worshippers, I lie submissively under the solitary apple tree in the kibbutz near a pack of black and white Canaan herding dogs. I know why they are here; they must protect the cows who are chewing their cud in the meadow, and they also guard the blossoming orange trees as the bees buzz around them in the utopian fields. After all, if Israel is the land of milk and honey, the dogs are aware that they must guard the cows and the groves that provide the food for this Promised Land.

As they watch over me, the dogs wag their tails in canine contentment and bask in the waning sunshine, surrounded by the aromas that only dogs can smell: fertile, sweet, promise-laden dreams of all the living and all the dead who did and who still desire to be one with their land, with their faith, with their loves. The scent of the shared dreams, both the failed and the realized, permeate the soft, lingering twilight air.

While I lie here bleeding, I watch my foals, filled with optimistic despair, nuzzle at the wind fallen fruit scattered around us. I shift uncomfortably from the pain in my ribs which does not ache as much as it did before the kibbutz's vet hastily applied pressure dressings to my wounds. I know why he worked so quickly; he did not want to be late for the Friday night prayer service. As I move again to find a more comfortable position, blood under the bandage ominously begins to seep into the ground.

The notes of the hymn "L' Dor V' Dor" (From Generation to Generation) sung responsively by the congregants of Kibbutz Issachar echo through the synagogue and triumphantly float across the valley. I slowly close my eyes while my three children struggle with one another over the one remaining uneaten apple lying under the tree. Golden shadows walk softly over my corpse as the sun sets in the west.

> *Fanatics have their dreams, wherewith they weave*
> *A paradise for a sect, the savage too*
> *From forth the loftiest fashion of his sleep*
> *Guesses at Heaven.*
>
> "Hyperion" by John Keats

ACKNOWLEDGMENTS

My sister-in-law Rebecca phoned us late one June night from Israel to tell us that an Egyptian spy had been surreptitiously following her for some 25 years without her knowledge. He first saw her while on an espionage mission prior to the 1956 war between Israel and his country, fell in love with her as he watched her referee a volleyball game between high school girls, and continued to watch over her. When she missed a bus one Friday afternoon in 1979, he knew she needed to go to Ashkelon to help her mother tend to her father who had just broken his leg. He convinced her to come into his cab and then showed her all the photos he had taken of her. She was amazed that he considered these photos good luck tokens which would ensure his safety if he were ever captured by Israelis. She was also upset that she had been totally unaware of his existence while he was literally eavesdropping upon her life. When they arrived at Ashkelon, he did kiss her hand and tell her to give her mother a "Good Sabbath wish." She never saw him again, but called my husband immediately to tell him the story of the spy who loved her. This novel would not exist if she had not given me permission to fictionalize her experience.

The careful reader will notice that I have used many quotations from Shakespeare's plays. I did ask him for permission to quote from many of his works, but he never answered my emails. Doubtlessly, he is too busy writing comedies for angelic audiences and tragedies for devils. I used information from Tom Robbins' marvelous book

Skinny Legs and All about Palés, the donkey deity. I did, however, see a dead donkey lying by the side of the road between Tel Aviv and Ashkelon while her bereft foal brayed piteously over her lifeless body, and I have never forgotten that sight.

The lyrics to "I'm Just a Girl Who Cain't Say No" are used with permission of the Rodgers-Hammerstein estate.

Mark Helprin has graciously allowed me to use the phrase "The powers of adhesion are determined by group particle affinity" from his book *Swan Lake* and I paraphrased the sentences that one has to be married for years to have a child, but make love only once if one is not married from his magnificent novel *A Soldier of the Great War*. He is a writer whose work I truly admire.

The chapter entitled "The Protocol of Sevres" contains material from the web site The Protocol of Sevres, 1956: Anatomy of a War Plot by Avi Shlaim, found at http://users.ox.ac.uk/~ssfc0005/ The%20Protocol%20of%20Sevres%201956%20Anatomy%20 of%20a%20War%20Plot.html. While my family and I visited the ancient ruins in Ashkelon, I also used information from the January, 2001 issue of *National Geographic* entitled "Ancient Ashkelon, Dead Men Do Tell Tales."

The story of the legendary self-sacrifice of the jeep driver Yehuda Kan Dror who drove his vehicle into the Egyptian army in the Mitla Pass formed the basis of my chapter in which my character David Silverman drove to his death to save his fellow paratroopers. The account of his heroic act can be found in the December 23, 2010, issue of Haaretz.com entitled "Into the Valley of Death." I also was aware of this incident when I watched Walter Cronkite cover the 1956 war on CBS television.

I found the information about Galla Placidia on the web site Ravenna Ville des mosaiques, Emilie Romagne buongiorno-italie. com and from Wikipedia. Fran Silber loaned me her copy of John Milton's *Samson Agonistes* whose play I thought would provide a far better venue for Rebecca and Ishmael to meet than the realistic one in which he became intrigued with her while she refereed a volley-ball game.

I have quoted one line "certain half-deserted streets and muttering retreats with insidious intent" from T. S. Eliot's poem "The Love Song of J. Alfred Prufrock," as well as parodied another line from the same poem, "I have measured out my life with coffee spoons." The last verse of the poem "Reluctance" is by Robert Frost and I parodied the last verse of "The Charge of the Light Brigade" by Alfred, Lord Tennyson. "Dover Beach" by Matthew Arnold also forms an important part of one chapter. "Foreign Children" is taken from Robert Louis Stevenson's collection of *A Child's Garden of Verses*.

The chapter about the moon watching Ishmael drive to Tel Aviv to betray Rebecca owes its tone to F. Scott Fitzgerald's novel *This Side of Paradise*.

I am indebted to Sally Sommers, who told me the miraculous story of her birth in a barn as her family fled from Poland during the Nazi invasion, and how a Polish farmer raised her until her parents were able to reclaim her after World War II ended.

I found much information about the military tactics during the 1956 war from Chaim Herzog's book *The Arab-Israeli Wars*. My husband told me the story about his escapade in the Novosibirsk train station when his family was returning from Russia to Poland after World War II. He did indeed think spaghetti reminded him of the poor train victim's legs when I cooked my first dish of linguine for him shortly after our marriage. He was also 6 years old when he bought the bar of soap which his mother buried when he brought it home.

I learned about MI6, Kim Philby and the Cambridge Five from many newspaper articles, films (especially the two of *Tinker, Tailor Soldier, Spy*) and television reports I have read and seen over the years about these double agents.

Gina Barr spent almost an entire summer editing this novel, and gave me tremendous encouragement. Her enthusiasm and her friendship are invaluable.

Also my sons Michael, Jonathan, and Ron contributed a great deal to the story. In fact, the first chapter is Jonathan's idea. Michael added many suggestions which gave the characters more dimension, and he was an invaluable editor.

My friend David Kanegis critiqued much of the script and made many valuable technical comments. My daughter-in-law Nina Didner was a gracious reader, who gave me many suggestions, and my friend Mary Last, who unfortunately passed away last October, also encouraged me to complete the manuscript. The writing group at Hemlock Farms, Pennsylvania, and in Lantana, Florida, led by Buck Buchanan gave me advice I sorely needed. I owe a tremendous debt to Carol Sharp, Marie Baccilli, and especially Sandy Jerinsky who also read my manuscript and is responsible for my inclusion of the three chapters detailing the emotions of Abraham, Sarah, and Hagar.

Above all, I must thank my editor, Shirin Wright, who spent many hours making sure every fact and every word is correct. She is a treasure whom I will always cherish.

And this book owes its existence to my acquisition editor Sean Jones who told me he loved how I intertwined the story of the contemporary Isaac and Rebecca with their biblical counterparts.

My thanks also to Emily Dueker of Inkwater Press who designed the cover and back page and spent many patient hours making sure this novel is printed accurately. Her ingenuity and patience are greatly valued. Many thanks also to Linda Franklin at Inkwater Press who also checked facts and formatted my novel so expertly.

Also, Alan Fleishman gave me tremendous advice and encouragement. I learned a great deal about the intricacies of book publishing from him.

Finally, I appreciate the immense patience of my hyperactive dog Macduff who forced himself to sit patiently for many, many hours by my feet as I typed away. Now he and I can freely roam the countryside while I contemplate the plot of my next novel. He does not realize that I spent most of my time writing this book, not at my computer, but on our hour-long walks as he chased every squirrel, ran after every deer, and barked at every turkey we met.

Lay on, Macduff. And blessed be you who can never love enough.

ABOUT THE AUTHOR

S andra Biber Didner teaches Literature and Composition at Palm
Beach State College in Lake Worth, Florida.

Family, book discussions, music, tennis, and above all, her
dogs, occupy most of her time when she is not reading, writing, or
teaching.

CPSIA information can be obtained
at www.ICGtesting.com
Printed in the USA
FFHW010748220319
51150851-56604FF